THE FURTHER
ADVENTURES OF

#2

THE FURTHER ADVENTURES OF

SOLAR PONS

#2

BASED ON THE CHARACTERS AND SERIES
CREATED BY AUGUST DERLETH

BASIL COPPER

EDITED BY STEPHEN JONES

DIP

Contents

vii   *The Editor's Note*

3   The Adventure of the Shaft of Death

77   The Adventure of the Baffled Baron

137   The Adventure of the Surrey Sadist

181   The Adventure of Missing Student

Editor's Note

*Unfortunately, while going through Basil Copper's papers, I
was unable to find any of his original manuscripts for the Solar
Pons stories. It is possible that these—along with all his
correspondence with August Derleth—were amongst the
uncatalogued material sent several years ago to the
Contemporary Collections repository of the Howard Gotlieb
Archival Research Center at Boston University.*

*We have therefore used the best sources available to us at
the present time, including existing texts hand-annotated by
the author himself, in the compilation of these volumes. I
have also taken the liberty—where required—of returning
his work to the English spellings and punctuation that the
author originally intended. SJ.*

THE FURTHER ADVENTURES OF

THE ADVENTURE OF
THE SHAFT OF DEATH

1

"YOU ARE UP early this morning, Parker?"

"Indeed, Pons. In fact I have been up all night on a difficult case and have only just come in."

"Ah, that accounts for the mud on your boots for it has only started raining within the last half-hour."

Solar Pons was in genial mood as he faced me in the sitting-room of our cosy quarters at 7B Praed Street, despite the rawness of the morning and the earliness of the hour. He waved me into a chair in front of the fire which Mrs. Johnson had already lit.

"You look all in, my dear fellow. Breakfast will be ready shortly."

"I shall do justice to it, Pons," I said. "You have something afoot, if I am not mistaken?"

"The conclusion of a small affair, Parker. The addition of a full-stop to a sentence as it were. I expect one call from Bancroft and if it gives me the news for which I have been waiting—that Karl Voss has been arrested in Holland—then I shall be satisfied."

He turned to the darkened window of the sitting-room, where the feeble rays of the street lamps were slowly being dispelled by the dawn, and tamped fresh tobacco into the bowl of his pipe.

"Though it means that I shall be at liberty again. And I confess that I find London confoundedly dull without the excitement of the chase."

"A little rest would do you good, Pons," said I. "You have been promising to accompany me to Scotland for some time."

"Pshaw, Parker, just look at it!"

Pons could not keep the disgust from his voice as he spread his hands to indicate the dismal sheets of rain falling outside the window.

"November is entirely the wrong time of year. And I prefer the capital. The sniffing out of evil-doing is holiday enough."

I closed my eyes and held out my hands to the warmth of the fireplace.

"I must confess that November is not the best time, Pons, but as your medical adviser as well as your friend, I must say you have been heavily overworking of late."

Solar Pons chuckled.

"Physician, heal thyself! I know you have the best intentions, my dear fellow, but just look at yourself this morning, grey with fatigue. If anyone overworks it is your average medical man. Why, I do not suppose you have had three straight days off in a row in the past year."

I snorted indignantly and opened my eyes. Solar Pons was standing in front of me, looking down with a whimsical expression on his face.

"If anyone needs a holiday it is you, Parker. My prescription for you is a fortnight at some Continental Spa. Or perhaps the winter sunshine of Nice."

"You are no doubt right, Pons," I grumbled. "And it is true

4

that I do need a holiday. But who is to pay for such a luxury as you describe is beyond my humble powers of ratiocination."

Pons smiled broadly.

"The King of Bavaria was unusually lavish in that little matter in which I was able to assist him, Parker. It was my intention that you should be my guest."

"It is extremely generous of you, Pons," I mumbled. "But I could not possibly permit it."

Solar Pons sat down at the breakfast table and looked at me musingly as I sprawled in the armchair.

"Well, if Scotland does not suit me and Monte Carlo does not suit you, we must content ourselves with some more modest programme of relaxation."

He broke off as Mrs. Johnson's well-scrubbed face with its heavy coils of hair looked interrogatively round the door. A pleasing aroma of fried bacon and hot coffee rose from the covered tray she carried.

"Come in, Mrs. Johnson, come along in," said Pons briskly, rising swiftly and opening the door for her. "You are indeed welcome this inclement November morning. Dr. Parker here is almost exhausted with his night's work. I have been trying to persuade him to take a brief holiday."

"I have been telling Dr. Parker that for months," said our good landlady, bustling about the table.

I rose from my position by the fire and swiftly retired to wash my hands. When I regained the sitting-room Mrs. Johnson had finished her preparations and Pons was pouring coffee for us from the silver-plated pot.

"Mrs. Johnson's diagnosis—and it is one with which I entirely concur—is a week at one of our spa towns, to be taken before the end of the month," said Pons decisively.

Mrs. Johnson smiled as I seated myself opposite Pons and reached for the toast.

"It is very good of you both to take such trouble over my health," I said mildly. "My locum would be quite agreeable, I have no doubt, and I am open to suggestions."

"Ah, we progress, Mrs. Johnson," said Pons briskly, rubbing his hands together. "This began with Parker trying to pack me off to Scotland in the current abominable weather and now we are prescribing for him."

"If you ask me, you are both in need of a holiday, Mr. Pons," said our landlady, quitting the room.

Pons looked quizzically after her as she closed the door and waited until she had descended the stairs.

"That admirable woman is right, you know, Parker," he said after a few minutes given over to the heaped plateful of food in front of him. "What say you to a modest jaunt?"

I put down my coffee cup in exasperation.

"It was I who suggested the holiday, Pons," I began with some asperity. "But I cannot really see us sitting in some dismal spa with a string orchestra playing, surrounded by gouty old gentlemen."

Solar Pons stroked his chin, little lines of humour showing at the corners of his mouth.

"You are right, Parker," he said. "You paint an horrific picture. We shall have to choose our venue with care."

And he said nothing further on the matter that morning. My medical duties took me out again after lunch and it was not until tea-time that I again set foot in our comfortable quarters. Pons was sitting in his mouse-coloured dressing gown and Mrs. Johnson had laid an occasional table up near the fire for high tea. I caught sight of crumpets, toasted teacakes, bread and butter and Madeira cake in my first glance and the expression on my face drew a dry chuckle from my companion.

"I told Mrs. Johnson you would no doubt be extremely weary by the time you came in, Parker, and I think that on this occasion she has excelled herself."

"Indeed, Pons," I said, sinking into an easy chair and allowing him to press a plate heaped with delicacies on me.

"You seem in ebullient mood," I added, when the keen edge of my appetite had been blunted.

"I have reason, Parker. I have just heard from Bancroft that Karl Voss was taken in Amsterdam early this morning. The case is closed."

"Congratulations, Pons. You will be free to take Mrs. Johnson's advice, then?"

"Why not, Parker? We have still to select a destination in which boredom may be safely kept at bay. If nothing in London intervenes, I shall be ready by Monday of next week."

"Very well, Pons," I said, stirring my tea. "I will make the arrangements with my locum."

"And in the meantime, my dear fellow, we have a gazetteer and an excellent selection of guidebooks on the shelf yonder. No, Parker, I think we will wait until after tea, if you please. I find that melted butter and art paper do not go well together."

⌐ 2

"**B**ath I think it is, then, Pons?"

The sitting-room was blue with tobacco-smoke and Pons and I, sprawled either side of the fire with whiskies at our elbows, had grown weary of the maps and guides which littered the table in front of us.

"It would appear to combine elegance and Roman antiquity with the benefits of urban entertainment such as can only be provided by a large city, Parker," said Pons languidly. "It is many years since I was last there and it is certainly one of the great cities of Europe. You are positively inspired this evening, my dear fellow."

"All I am worried about is whether we can get away in time, Pons," I said. "I have arranged things with my locum and it would be annoying, not to say disappointing, if I had to cancel."

Pons raised his eyebrows.

"I do not follow you, Parker."

"Now you are being obtuse, Pons," I could not resist saying. "Are you really telling me that if an interesting case arises before Monday, you will turn it down?"

Solar Pons smiled a thin smile as he took the pipe from his mouth.

"A point, Parker, a definite point. You are developing quite a pawky sense of humour of late."

He blew out a cloud of aromatic blue smoke and eyed me seriously.

"My dear fellow, I have given you my word. We have both been stretching ourselves. I guarantee that we will be on that train on Monday morning."

With that I had to rest content but I must confess I spent an uneasy weekend, only really relaxing on Monday, when we were safely ensconced with our luggage in the taxi on the way to Paddington. It was a dry, sunny day and my spirits rose considerably. Pons too was unusually affected by the weather and even hummed a bar or two of a popular air in a tuneless monotone until I begged him to desist.

We lunched on the train and I watched the rich countryside

unfold beyond the windows in a euphoric dream, conscious that Pons was again buried in his magazine and making elaborate calculations in pencil on its margin. In mid-afternoon we descended at Bath Spa Station and hailed a taxi. It was a bright, dry day still with scudding clouds and Pons looked with satisfaction at the Georgian buildings of the creamy local stone as we drove up Manvers Street and onward to the Grand Parade, leaving the massive pile of the Abbey on our left.

The taxi turned right over the elegant Pulteney Bridge with its shops in the style of Florence and Pons looked at the foaming race of Pulteney Weir as we crossed the Avon, the scale of the city slowly being revealed to us.

"I was not mistaken, Parker," said Solar Pons with satisfaction. "Roman Bath. Still one of the most elegant cities of Europe, I think."

"Undoubtedly, Pons," I replied. "I trust you will find much to occupy you here."

"The prospect certainly seems a little less arid than it did in Praed Street a few hours ago," Pons conceded drily. "Though whether I shall think so at the end of a week spent in these Georgian surroundings is another matter."

"Come, Pons," I said with some asperity. "This is my holiday too. We must just make the best of it."

"You make it sound a penance, Parker," said Solar Pons with a wry laugh as the taxi passed through Aura Place and pulled up at an imposing hotel in Great Pulteney Street. Our rooms were ready and after we had registered and unpacked, I met Pons in the lobby and suggested afternoon tea at the Pump Room.

"I must say, Parker, you are throwing yourself into the role quite thoroughly. But it sounds a not unpleasant idea."

He consulted his watch.

"It is just after four. An apposite hour."

Before we could leave the lobby, however, there was an interruption, as the receptionist came over from her rosewood desk at one side of the spacious entrance.

"Mr. Pons? This just came for you, Mr. Pons."

I looked at Pons resignedly as the girl handed him the telegram.

"Not bad news, Pons?"

Solar Pons' lean face lit up and he rubbed his hands together briskly.

"Good news, Parker. It seems that my services are needed."

He handed me the form. It was addressed Pons, c/o Hotel Glendale and simply said: MUST CONSULT YOU MATTER LIFE AND DEATH. 8 P.M. THIS EVENING YOUR HOTEL. SEPTIMUS GRIMPTON.

I sighed and handed the form back to Pons.

"This is supposed to be a holiday, Pons."

"Is it not, Parker."

Solar Pons looked at me sideways in a conspiratorial manner as we descended the steps of the hotel and set off in the direction of the centre of Bath. It was dusk and lamps were blooming along the broad vista of Great Pulteney Street and the grace and symmetry of the houses made one think we were back in the eighteenth century.

"Who on earth is Septimus Grimpton, Pons?"

"Your guess is as good as mine, Parker. I have never heard of the man."

"He has certainly heard of you, Pons," I said somewhat bitterly. "And how did he know you were staying here?"

"Possibly the good Mrs. Johnson released our address in Bath, Parker."

I shook my head.

"That is a great pity, Pons."

"On the contrary, my dear Parker, Mrs. Johnson was merely following out instructions."

"But we have just arrived, Pons," I protested. "And if you have to return to London..."

"My dear fellow, I shall not be returning to London. If Mr. Grimpton is calling at our hotel, is it not likely that he lives or has business in this neighbourhood? I hardly fancy that he would travel all this way from London just to consult me, especially when Mrs. Johnson would have acquainted him with the fact that it is my holiday."

I stared at Pons for a moment as we crossed the bridge over the Avon and turned left into Grand Parade.

"That puts a different complexion on the matter, Pons."

"Does it not, Parker. And now let us absorb the unique atmosphere of this extraordinary city. Observe the almost magical way in which the Abbey rises from the dusk. If I am not much mistaken England's first Archbishop began its building."

We crossed the street and wandered through the precincts to where the lights of the Pump Room beckoned from the shadows. The area was crowded with shoppers and tourists and the red afterglow of the sun yet lingered in the west, turning the upper stones of the ancient Abbey Towers to carmine.

The rococo splendour of the Pump Room engulfed us and as we sat waiting for the buxom waitress to bring us tea, Pons glanced round the vast hall with its Chippendale furniture, absorbed in his study of the faces of the people who sipped their tea or ate their Bath buns, while their conversation rose like the murmur of the sea to the high ceiling far overhead.

An eight-piece orchestra on a dais at the far end of the huge room struck up a Strauss waltz and Pons turned back to me with an ironic smile.

"You are in your element now, Parker."

I waited until the waitress had put down the tea-tray, conscious of the toasted crumpets and other delicacies that were spread out on its silver surface.

"You must confess that it has a certain charm, Pons."

Pons nodded.

"Oh, I give you that, my dear fellow. As a holiday it has much to commend it. As a way of life it would soon pall."

"I could not agree more, Pons," I said. "But as we are on holiday let us just enjoy it."

And with that I bit with satisfaction into my first crumpet.

3

We were sitting in the lounge of the hotel at a quarter past eight when a page-boy came in, followed by an elderly man dressed in a thick overcoat with a fur collar.

"Ah, Parker," said Pons, rising from his place by the fire. "That should be the mysterious Mr. Grimpton if I mistake not."

It was indeed for the old gentleman gave a start as he caught sight of Pons' lean, tall figure, dismissed the page-boy with a coin and hurried toward us through a sea of leather armchairs.

"Mr. Solar Pons? It is indeed good of you to see me on your holiday, my dear sir. As you will have guessed, I am Septimus Grimpton."

"Pray sit down, Mr. Grimpton. You will find this seat nearest the fire more comfortable."

Our visitor seated himself, unbuttoning his coat.

"I hope my telegram did not inconvenience you, Mr. Pons,

particularly as I understand this is the first day of your holiday."

"Not at all, Mr. Grimpton. I gather that it is a serious matter on which you wish to consult me. This is my friend and colleague, Dr. Lyndon Parker."

"Delighted to meet you, doctor."

Septimus Grimpton rose from his chair and gave me a half-bow as he seized my hand. He was a man of some seventy years of age, though of vigorous aspect and with a rosy complexion almost like that of a child. He had snow-white hair which hung over his forehead in careless wisps, and his tufted eyebrows waved in comic manner behind his gold pince-nez as he talked. One of the most striking things about him was his vivid blue eyes which made his face come wonderfully alive.

Pons had gone to stand by the fireplace and was studying our visitor with more than usual interest.

"A countryman and a scholar I see, Mr. Grimpton. One used to taking notes in public places such as libraries or the rooms of learned institutions."

"Why yes, Mr. Pons. You know me?"

The blue eyes had swivelled in an arresting manner to hold Pons in their unwavering stare. Solar Pons shook his head with a smile.

"You are of vigorous build and your complexion denotes the man who is much in the open air. Yet there is something of the scholar about your manner and tone of voice. When I find that combined with the slight stoop which comes from hours spent over books I deduce a gentleman of scholarly pursuits."

"And the libraries and institutions, Pons?" I could not resist putting in.

Solar Pons chuckled.

"Mr. Grimpton is dressed expensively and in perfect taste.

Yet I see from his high quality overcoat that the cuff of the right arm is nevertheless frayed and ink-stained. That comes only from his habit of resting his forearm on a table or desk while writing."

"But the public institutions, Pons?" I persisted.

Solar Pons shook his head and made a slight clicking noise with his tongue.

"You know my methods, Parker. It is only in public institutions or libraries, where conditions are often chill in winter-time, that the searcher after knowledge would keep his overcoat on."

I gave our visitor a wry smile.

"There is no catching you out, Pons."

"You do me too much honour, Parker. But you have not corroborated my findings, Mr. Grimpton."

Our visitor shifted in his chair and his eyes sparkled behind the pince-nez.

"It is only because I am struck dumb with admiration, Mr. Pons. You are correct in every respect. It is obvious my confidence in coming to you is not misplaced."

"You live in the neighbourhood, Mr. Grimpton?"

"At Penderel Parva, Mr. Pons, a small village just outside Bath; in fact, only half an hour's drive from here."

"Might I ask how you discovered my whereabouts?"

"That is just it, Mr. Pons. A wonderful stroke of fortune. I was at my wit's end. I was so worried about this bizarre affair that I was about to set out for London to seek your advice. But some providence made me first telephone your London address and the good lady there told me you were staying in Bath and very kindly provided the name of your hotel. I am so sorry to cut into your holiday with my problems."

"I am at your disposal, Mr. Grimpton," said Pons. "Other

people's problems are my holiday so far as I am concerned and you seem to have your share of them if your telegram is anything to go by."

"You are too kind, Mr. Pons. I think I can promise you something out of the ordinary. And money is no object."

Pons held up his hand.

"I never discuss terms, Mr. Grimpton. I have a fixed fee and I never deviate from it, save when I remit it altogether."

Our visitor smiled gently at Pons and pushed his straggling white locks back from his eyes.

"My apologies, gentlemen. And now, to the purpose of my visit."

Septimus Grimpton's face had changed now and he had a strange, bleak look in his eyes that suddenly made one aware of his age.

"I live at Penderel Lodge, sir, a large house of a rambling nature, in extensive grounds outside the village of Penderel Parva," he commenced.

"It was built by my grandfather, Sennacherib Grimpton, a notable eccentric of Bath and a man who had money and taste but whose later life was clouded by his growing miserliness and a number of tragic events, which began with the premature death of his wife, my grandmother."

Grimpton gave a deferential smile and added, "I mention all this in some detail, Mr. Pons, because I wish you to have the background of this strange affair firmly in your mind."

"Pray go on, Mr. Grimpton."

"My life has been lived much out of the world, Mr. Pons, though in earlier years I travelled extensively on the continent in pursuit of my scholarly and bibliophile interests. I have one of the finest libraries in the West of England. A bachelor, I live with my secretary and domestic staff at Penderel Lodge, which descended to me on the death of my father some eighteen years ago. So much for detail, Mr. Pons."

Solar Pons leaned casually against the mantel, his deep-set eyes fixed unwaveringly upon our visitor.

"The strange events at Penderel Lodge began some eight months ago, Mr. Pons. They are a complete mystery to me, to my housekeeper, Mrs. Shipton; and to my secretary, Jocelyn Granger. There were strange noises in the night; footsteps; doors slamming in the dead hours. I was several times disturbed and made the rounds of the house but was never able to find anything amiss.

"Then things took a more serious turn. We have had several burglaries, Mr. Pons..."

Solar Pons made a low clicking noise with his tongue and held up his hand.

"Pray be precise as to detail, Mr. Grimpton."

The blue eyes swivelled from me to my companion.

"Well, Mr. Pons, none of it makes much sense. About three months ago I was aroused one night by a loud crash. Both Mrs. Shipton and myself made a search but were unable to discover any intruder in the house. But we discovered a number of books in my library had slipped to the floor. We questioned my secretary and the servants in the morning but no one knew anything about it."

Solar Pons pulled at the lobe of his ear in the manner long familiar to me and stared reflectively at our guest.

"Could the books have collapsed from the shelves of their own accord?"

"It is barely possible, Mr. Pons, for the shelves are raked slightly backward to prevent just that."

16

"What were the volumes?"

"Nothing of importance, Mr. Pons. Merely bound records relating to the estate in my grandfather's time. Worth nothing in monetary terms."

"I see. Please go on."

"There have been two burglaries since, Mr. Pons. One, a month after the incident just mentioned. I saw lights coming from my study on this occasion. They shone on my blind and awoke me. I must have disturbed someone because I found the French windows open and a number of things missing."

"You reported this to the police?"

"Certainly, Mr. Pons. But nothing followed. It was a dry night and there were no footprints on the terrace."

"What had been stolen?"

"That was the ridiculous part of it, Mr. Pons. Quite worthless things. A bronze ashtray from my desk; a pair of candle-snuffers; and a pewter vase principally."

Pons' eyes sparkled.

"This grows more interesting by the minute, Mr. Grimpton. What say you, Parker?"

"Indeed, Pons," I returned. "An amateur sort of thief by the sound of it."

"Undoubtedly. Unless he intended to corner the bronze and pewter market."

Our visitor's eyes widened.

"I hardly think so, Mr. Pons. But I confess I am unable to make anything of this."

Solar Pons quitted the mantel and sat down opposite our visitor.

"There was another burglary at the house three weeks ago. Just as pointless as the first. I slept through this but my secretary awoke and chased an intruder on the terrace. He was shortly joined by my housekeeper but the man got clean away. A few trinkets from the morning room were taken and there was some disturbance in the library but nothing of value was stolen. The rare books are kept in locked cabinets. They would have been worth a fortune to any thief."

"But that is a highly specialised department," said Solar Pons enigmatically. "And calls for esoteric knowledge unlikely to be possessed by many. Hence the relatively few rare book thieves in operation on a world scale."

"I must bow to your arcane knowledge of the subject, Mr. Pons," said our visitor ironically. "At least it has relieved part of my mind."

"That completes your sequence of strange events, Mr. Grimpton?" began Solar Pons. "You mentioned life and death . . . "

"Except for this morning's incident," our visitor interrupted. "The inhabitants of Penderel Lodge are in a state of terror, Mr. Pons."

"Something of the utmost gravity has happened then?"

Septimus Grimpton nodded.

"Murder in the most shocking form, Mr. Pons, under the most bizarre circumstances."

4

There was a long silence in the quiet of the hotel lounge. From beyond the thick-curtained windows the soft humming of a motor vehicle rose and then receded as it glided down Great Pulteney Street and turned into Aura Place.

Pons' face was grim. He leaned forward and tented his fingers before him as he stared at Grimpton.

"Pray be most precise and careful as to detail, Mr. Grimpton."

"Certainly, Mr. Pons. Though I am most shaken by such a terrible incident occurring in my grounds. A gardener was coming on duty at six o' clock when he had occasion to pass near the Mausoleum. There is a tarmacadam drive there and he was shocked and horrified to see bloodied footprints on the carriageway."

Our client's voice had dropped to a low whisper and he stared at Pons with a suddenly haggard face.

"Bizarre and shocking, Pons," I said.

Solar Pons nodded.

"Bizarre indeed, Parker. What is this Mausoleum you spoke of, Mr. Grimpton?"

"Another whim of my eccentric grandfather, Mr. Pons. When my grandmother died he had a fancy to build a Mausoleum in the grounds of the estate. She is buried there in a marble sarcophagus. He is also interred within the Mausoleum."

"There is an agreeably Gothic tone to your story, Mr. Grimpton, if you do not mind me saying so."

Our visitor nodded.

"A little too Gothic and a little too grim for my taste, Mr. Pons. As I was saying, the gardener found these footprints. A few hundred yards farther on, in a small grove of trees fronting the house, he discovered a roughly-dressed man, terribly injured. He was covered in blood, which was dripping from a large wound in his chest. How he had survived that long was a miracle. The house was aroused, the police and a doctor summoned, but he died within half an hour of the latter's arrival, despite all that he could do."

"Was he able to say anything?"

"Just one thing, Mr. Pons. He mumbled something to Hoskins, the gardener. It was something about 'The Shaft of Death'. He repeated this strange phrase three or four times before he died. Nothing else."

Solar Pons sat in silence for a moment, rapt in thought.

"Had the weapon been found, Mr. Grimpton?"

The old man shook his head.

"That is another of the weird things, Mr. Pons. I have not finished yet. The bloodied footprints were traced back from the roadway by Inspector Morgan and his men. They led to the Mausoleum, Mr. Pons, which had been entered with a key, which was still in the lock. There was a good deal of blood within the building, particularly on the marble paving on which the tomb of my grandmother stands. There were bloodied hand-marks on the front of the marble effigy which surmounts the sarcophagus. There the trail ended."

"Say rather there it began," murmured Pons. "Well, Mr. Grimpton, I have seldom listened to a more grisly or more baffling story. Have you more to tell me?"

"Very little, Mr. Pons. The dead man has been identified. He was Abel Stokoe, a rough character who formerly made his living as a prizefighter. He was a convicted felon and in fact had been released from prison only three months ago."

"I see."

Solar Pons rose from his seat and paced silently up and down in front of the fireplace.

"He was sent to prison for what, Mr. Grimpton?"

"According to Inspector Morgan, Mr. Pons, for a number of offences. Occasioning grievous bodily harm; but mostly for house-breaking."

Solar Pons made a little clicking noise with his tongue.

"What do you make of it, Mr. Pons?"

Our visitor sat with his head on one side, regarding my companion anxiously.

"Nothing as yet, Mr. Grimpton. But one should not waste too much time in these cases. If you have no objection, Parker, I should like to go over the ground tonight."

"Certainly, Pons."

Pons glanced at the great cased clock which ticked away in a corner of the lounge.

"It wants only a few minutes to nine o'clock. If you have your car at the door, Mr. Grimpton, there is no time like the present."

"Thank you, Mr. Pons. You have taken a great weight off my mind."

Septimus Grimpton rose and shook Solar Pons' hand effusively.

"We will talk further in the car on the way to your house, Mr. Grimpton."

It was indeed only a short journey to Penderel Lodge and after crossing the Avon, Mr. Grimpton's gleaming Rolls-Royce, driven by a taciturn chauffeur, glided its way through undulating countryside to the small village of Penderel Parva. Passing through the village, the vehicle turned in through ornamental iron gates that led to a sizeable park.

The journey had passed with Pons' monosyllabic questions and Mr. Grimpton's necessarily longer and more detailed answers but now Pons seemed satisfied with his questioning and the church clock had barely finished marking half-past nine before our host's massive vehicle crunched to a halt in the curving driveway which stretched like a white ribbon before us in the light of the moon.

It was a cold night and I was glad of my thick overcoat as Pons sprang down impatiently, his pocket torch in his hand.

"This is the spot?"

"Just ahead, Mr. Pons. The police had canvas laid to preserve the prints, though it is obvious what happened."

Grimpton led the way to a spot about five yards distant, now brightly illuminated by the headlamps of the Rolls-Royce. Pons quickly unrolled the canvas and I could not repress a slight shiver at the bloodied outlines of the boot-marks thus revealed. Pons quickly worked his way over the ground, his pocket lens out, while his torch occasionally supplemented the beams of the headlamps.

He made an impatient clicking noise with his tongue.

"A great pity, Mr. Grimpton. The boots of the constabulary habitually obliterate that which should be preserved."

"What on earth do you mean, Mr. Pons?"

"It does not really matter on this occasion, Mr. Grimpton. But if there had been indications of another person on the tarmacadam they would undoubtedly have been effaced by the eager shoe-marks of the Inspector's gaping assistants."

Pons turned his lean, hawk-like face toward our host.

"Incidentally, why did you not leave this matter to the official police, Mr. Grimpton?"

The old scholar hesitated, a strange expression on his face.

"It seemed to me that there was something here beyond the purview of the normal," he said.

"Something that might affect your family?"

Septimus Grimpton smiled faintly.

"You are an extremely shrewd man, Mr. Pons. This business of the family vault, for example."

Pons stood with one hand pulling at the lobe of his ear.

"You may rely on my discretion, Mr. Grimpton. Providing that it sits four-square with my conscience."

"That is understood, Mr. Pons."

Grimpton signalled to his chauffeur and the man brought the car up while Pons replaced the canvas over the driveway. The headlamp beams were now slewed across the park and Pons followed the trail of footprints, easily distinguished now in the soft grass. They ended on a knoll, among the grove of trees our host had already spoken of. Pons knelt, his torch-beam steady on the thick, dark patch of blood still visible on the ground, indicating the spot where the unfortunate Stokoe had died.

He rose to his feet, putting the lens away, while his deep-set eyes looked across to the façade of the gracious house that fronted us across the parkland, its bulk bleached silver in the moonlight.

"The sequence of events seems perfectly clear, Mr. Grimpton. The man was evidently making for the house after the brutal attack on him. What did the police say about the cause of death?"

Grimpton led the way back down from the knoll in the direction from which we had come, while the car reversed until it was pointed toward the main gates.

"A massive wound over the heart, Mr. Pons. Apparently inflicted with some semi-sharp instrument wielded with considerable force. Dr. Kellett said it was incredible Stokoe had survived so long."

"How could he have got into the grounds?"

"There are many places along the boundary, Mr. Pons. Hedges, or even high walls will not keep such people out."

"Very true, Mr. Grimpton. I should like to see this family Mausoleum of yours before we go to the house."

"Certainly, Mr. Pons."

We had entered the car by this time and our host tapped on the glass partition; the Rolls-Royce glided back down the driveway and then took a secondary fork to the left which wound uphill through dark belts of trees. At length we came to a wide concourse and the trees dropped away. The beams of the headlights picked out a large octagonal building of white marble which seemed to shimmer like bone in the moonlight.

"That is the Mausoleum, gentlemen," said Grimpton in a hushed voice.

5

Pons descended from our vehicle and rapidly crossed over to the marble steps of the white building which was of tremendous size. We waited before the palatial bronze doors in the rising wind as Septimus Grimpton hurried after us. The chauffeur again brought the Rolls-Royce as far up toward the steps as was practicable until the beams illuminated the doorway.

Grimpton produced a large bronze key and inserted it into the lock.

"The police have finished their investigations here, Mr. Pons," he murmured. "I have told the Inspector I was engaging your services and he said I could not have done better."

"That is extremely flattering, Mr. Grimpton," said Pons gravely, shooting me a swift glance.

He put his hand to the portal which went easily round with a barely perceptible squeak.

"How often is this place entered, Mr. Grimpton?"

Our client hesitated.

"Perhaps once or twice a year, Mr. Pons," he replied. "There was some small memorial ceremony in my father's time, which has persisted in latter years."

"Your parents are not interred here?"

A startled look passed across Grimpton's face, accentuated by the yellow light of the headlamp beams.

"Certainly not, Mr. Pons," he said sharply. "They did not subscribe to my grandfather's eccentricities. They are buried in a village churchyard in Devonshire."

Solar Pons had his pocket torch out and was examining the hinges of the giant door.

"I ask only because of the state of these doors, Mr. Grimpton. They have been recently greased."

"That is indeed strange, Mr. Pons. I will question my outdoor staff if you think it important."

"It is of the utmost significance," said Solar Pons mysteriously. "Eh, Parker?"

I blinked.

"If you say so, Pons."

Solar Pons smiled enigmatically and directed his torch beam on to the interior of the Mausoleum. It was indeed a curious chamber in which we found ourselves; beyond the spacious entrance whose bronze vases set within niches had obviously once contained flowers, there was a large circular room about thirty feet wide. Our footsteps echoed heavily under the domed ceiling as we went slowly over the marble inlaid paving, which bore rich, incised patterns in green and gold. There were no windows and the lights of the car from outside, and the beams from Pons' torch, cast strange and sombre shadows which fled across the white walls.

The bloodied footprints, of which brief traces remained on the steps outside, were again visible here, and Pons gave a little catch of his breath as he followed them back with his torch.

"What do you make of it, Parker?"

I bent down to examine the markings more closely.

"Why, that he was struck somewhere within the Mausoleum, Pons?"

"Excellent, Parker. As a medical man I was sure that fact would not escape you."

"How so, Mr. Pons?" put in Septimus Grimpton.

"Because, as so often happens, Mr. Grimpton, the wound did not commence to bleed at once. It was only afterward, as he began to walk, that the blood pumped more vigorously through his veins, and copious bleeding began, outside the Mausoleum."

There was a heavy silence as our client absorbed this information. It was broken by Pons, who went forward to a raised dais in the centre of the chamber. It bore the sarcophagus of Septimus Grimpton's grandmother if the marble female effigy sculptured on top was a true indication.

The plinth carried the inscription, in heavy chiselled letters: EPHROSINA GRIMPTON 1780—1855. And underneath, in flowing script lettering: TURN DOWN AN EMPTY GLASS.

"An unusual inscription, Pons," I began.

"A quotation from the *The Rubáiyát of Omar Khayyám*, Parker," said Pons. "The final stanza in Fitzgerald's translation, if I am not mistaken. It refers to the ephemerality of all human hopes and aspirations, Parker. But it is a strange epitaph for the mid-Victorian period, I agree. Your grandfather was an unusual man, Mr. Grimpton."

"Indeed, Mr. Pons," said the old scholar, looking at my companion with intense blue eyes. "I did not think the quotation would escape you. Though of ripe years, my grandmother died in a riding accident."

Pons was silent for a few moments, carefully examining the

plinth of the sarcophagus and the surrounding floor, which also bore traces of blood-flecks. The plinth was set in the midst of a circular pattern and I followed it round when Pons gave another brief exclamation. I followed the dancing beam of the torch and saw the bloodied imprints of two hands on the feet of the white marble figure.

"I would venture to say that Stokoe was struck somewhere about here, Mr. Grimpton. He first put his hand to his breast, where he had been wounded, and carried the first traces of blood to the effigy here as he leaned against it to recover himself."

"He must have been a man of tremendous strength, Mr. Pons."

"I am inclined to agree, Mr. Grimpton."

Pons looked round curiously.

"But I must confess there are some aspects which puzzle me. I find no trace of a second person, the man who struck the blow. Yet he must have been close beside his victim. And why did he not strike him again to finish him?"

"Ah, there I cannot follow you, Mr. Pons," said our client respectfully, stepping back to the edge of the plinth and lapsing into silence.

"That is your grandfather over there?"

Pons' dancing torch-beam passed on to indicate a smaller effigy, set against the far wall; this carried only a plain marble tablet with the name and dates.

"Simple and dignified," said Pons. "He evidently thought a great deal of your grandmother."

"He worshipped her, Mr. Pons. He was buried there according to the wishes expressed in his will. Though wanting to be near her within the Mausoleum, he did not want her disturbed for his interment. In fact, Mr. Pons, the raised platform is symbolic, or so my father said. It partakes, in some ways, of the mediaeval."

Pons nodded.

"The allusion had not escaped me, Mr. Grimpton. When the inferior in rank slept at the feet of their lord or lady. A rather charming sentiment for the high-tide of the Victorian age."

"You are a man of great sensitivity, Mr. Pons."

Pons acknowledged the compliment with a slight bow and his gaze once again raked round the strange chamber in which we found ourselves.

"I think we have seen everything of importance here, Mr. Grimpton. A short visit to your house will put most of the salient points within my orbit."

"Certainly, Mr. Pons."

We waited outside while the old man locked the great bronze doors behind us.

"How many keys are there to this door, Mr. Grimpton?"

"About three, I think, Mr. Pons," said Grimpton as we once again re-entered the car and the chauffeur reversed it and set off toward the house.

"And where are they kept?"

"There are two in my study and a third in the estate manager's office, Mr. Pons. We keep the building clean, of course, and it is entered for that purpose from time to time."

Pons nodded.

"So that if anyone could abstract the key it would be only the work of a moment to make an impression of it."

"No doubt, Mr. Pons, but for what purpose eludes me."

"That is what makes these little problems so intriguing," said Pons with a thin smile. "Pray give me the benefit of your thoughts on the matter, Parker."

"Well, Pons," I said. "Supposing it had been robbery. Thieves falling out, say."

"I am not usually obtuse, Parker, but on this occasion I do not quite follow you."

"The materials of the vault, Pons. The marble flooring and other fittings; the bronze doors themselves, would be extremely valuable."

Solar Pons leaned forward and toyed with the lobe of his ear, his face heavy with thought.

"Distinctly ingenious, Parker. You excel yourself, but I think not. While such a theory might be plausible in a metropolis like London it would hardly suffice out here in the country. And while it is true to say that the materials are extremely valuable, think of all the time and trouble. It would need tools, equipment, many men; to say nothing of a large vehicle to transport such booty away. Yet there are no tyre-marks in the grounds at all that I have been able to discover. And I have particularly looked for such markings. I fear we must look elsewhere for the explanation of this bizarre affair."

Pons turned to our client.

"And we must not forget also, Mr. Grimpton, that unless Stokoe were raving, he must have meant something by his enigmatic reference to 'The Shaft of Death'. I would submit it referred to the method of his own demise. He repeated it not once but several times, according to your story."

"Perfectly correct, Mr. Pons."

"This is a heavy problem, Pons," I said. "And will need all your ratiocinative gifts."

"Will it not, Parker," said Pons with an enigmatic glance at both of us. And he said nothing further until we were inside the house.

6

As our client had indicated, Penderel Lodge was a rambling old place, but furnished lavishly with taste and discernment. Septimus Grimpton had made certain improvements in the matter of creature comforts and I for one was extremely grateful for the enormous fire which blazed in the great panelled hall to which Grimpton immediately led us on arrival at the house.

The door had been opened by a grave-faced butler with a fringe of white hair at the temples and now he brought whisky in a decanter, together with crystal goblets on a silver tray.

"Pray make yourselves comfortable, gentlemen."

The butler had poured the drinks and we stood agreeably engaged by the mellow flames of the fire when our host recalled the man, who was on the point of leaving the room.

"Are the police still here, Simmons?"

The butler inclined his head, the lights from the chandeliers glinting silver at his temples.

"The main body have returned to Bath this afternoon, sir. Inspector Morgan is working on his notes in the morning room. It was his intention, I believe, to await your return."

"Very well, Simmons. We will see the Inspector in a few minutes. Will you ask Mr. Granger to step this way if he has not retired for the night."

"Certainly, Mr. Grimpton."

Our host rubbed his hands together and turned to us, his blue eyes frank and level.

"Mrs. Shipton, my housekeeper, and Hoskins, the gardener, are available for questioning should you desire to have them here."

Pons looked across at the great grandfather clock in the corner.

"It is past ten, Mr. Grimpton. I do not think I will bother them tonight. There will be time enough tomorrow."

"As you wish, Mr. Pons."

There came a low rapping at the door and at our host's command a thin, sandy-haired fellow pushed open the door and stood poised upon the threshold. He had an alert expression on his face and his body was coiled like a tense spring so that he reminded me of nothing so much as a wire-haired terrier.

"Little of import to announce, Mr. Grimpton," he said easily. "Inspector Morgan is no farther forward, I feel."

"That may well be," said Septimus Grimpton drily, "but I think we must forbear to sit in judgement on the police force until they have had longer on the case. Granger, this is Dr. Lyndon Parker and Mr. Solar Pons, who has come to give us the benefit of his great deductive wisdom in the matter."

The secretary smiled, showing even white teeth, and hurried over to shake hands with each of us in turn.

"Welcome, gentlemen. I am a great admirer of your methods, Mr. Pons."

"Let us just hope that you will remain an admirer after my departure, Mr. Granger," said Solar Pons good-humouredly. "I understand you played a leading part in these mysterious events."

A shadow passed across the secretary's face. At Grimpton's invitation he poured himself a steep measure of whisky and went to stand moodily by the fireplace, facing Pons.

"I do not know what Mr. Grimpton has told you, Mr. Pons. I chased somebody one evening, yes. But I know as little as anyone else about these strange events. And as for the shocking murder this morning, I cannot for the life of me make any sense of the matter."

31

"Then you are at one with Dr. Parker here," said Pons wryly. "But logic has a way of imparting coherence to otherwise widely disconnected events. We have a series of burglaries or attempted burglaries, in each of which valueless trifles were stolen. We have a murder and a Mausoleum; no visible weapon and a mysterious death-cry of a man evidently of sound mind, for he repeated the same phrase several times."

I shook my head.

"Baffling complexity, Pons."

"Is it not, Parker?" observed Solar Pons mischievously. "But light will break in, I have no doubt, as we proceed."

The secretary shook his head, exchanging a glance with his employer.

"Well, sir, I am entirely at your disposal, if you wish to question me. Similarly, the contents of the study and my own records are freely available. With Mr. Grimpton's permission, of course."

Solar Pons had seated himself in a deep leather chair at the side of the fireplace and now he tented his fingers before him, his sharp eyes fixed unwaveringly on the secretary's face.

"Well, that is good to know, Mr. Granger. I shall not trouble you this evening, but I may have need of your views and your records at some future time."

"They will be ready, Mr. Pons."

"What do you make of this man, Stokoe, Mr. Granger?"

The secretary shook his head, swilling the amber liquid around in his glass.

"I had never heard of the fellow until today, Mr. Pons. Though he sounds a nasty character, by all accounts. Inspector Morgan has some theory about gypsies, so we may learn something further."

"Indeed."

Solar Pons pursed his lips and looked inquiringly at our host.

"There is a band of gypsies encamped on the far side of the village," said Grimpton shortly. "Though what connection they may have had with the man Stokoe only the Inspector knows."

"Perhaps we had better ask him," said Solar Pons, rising easily from his chair and bidding the secretary goodnight.

"Bring your glasses along by all means, gentlemen," said Grimpton with a good-natured smile. "We will not stand on ceremony at a time like this."

I hurried after Pons and Grimpton, for my friend had strode out across the parquet in his usual dynamic manner.

"The door on the far side of the hall, Mr. Pons," Grimpton called after him.

I gained the threshold in time to see a heavily-built, middle-aged man dressed in comfortable tweeds rise from a desk near the fire with a welcoming smile. The butler, Simmons, was standing in front of the desk as though in the act of being questioned and I noticed a notebook covered in inked longhand script on the desk, with the police officer's silver pen beside it.

"Morgan, Mr. Pons. Inspector, Bath C.I.D. An honour to have you here, sir."

Pons shook hands, his eyes sharply scrutinising the Inspector's face.

"You honour me, Inspector. Rhondda Valley, I should say. You are a member of the Metropolitan Police Hockey Club. Enthusiastic rugby player too, I believe."

The Inspector's mouth was wide open.

"Correct, Mr. Pons. Though how..."

"Tut, it was simple enough," interrupted Solar Pons.

"I have made some study of accents. That lilting speech with its curious inflection is found nowhere else but in the Rhondda Valley. Your tie denotes your membership of the hockey club."

"Ah, Mr. Pons."

The Inspector smiled again. "I was a member for years when I served in London. I retain my membership. But my enthusiasm for rugby?"

"Your nose has been broken not once, but twice, Inspector. And..."

"That could have occurred in a number of sports, including boxing," I could not resist putting in mischievously.

"As I was about to add, Parker, if you would kindly refrain from interrupting me," Solar Pons went on blandly, "I have twice had the pleasure of seeing Mr. Morgan perform as centre-half at Twickenham in earlier years. So my observations on the matter were based on knowledge and not on the evidence of his nose, though the breaks are typical of the type of blow dealt by a hand-off."

Inspector Morgan's expression denoted amusement as he caught sight of my discomfiture but Solar Pons, ignoring the butler and Grimpton, who stood somewhat awkwardly by the fire, went on easily, "What do you make of all this, Inspector?"

Morgan shook his head and resumed his seat at the desk.

"I have not come to any definite conclusions, Mr. Pons."

"That is always wise at an early stage of such an investigation," said Pons, going to sit on a leather divan where I shortly joined him.

"But you must have some sort of theory. The Mausoleum and Stokoe, for instance?"

The Inspector wrinkled up his brow in furrows of concentration.

"It's a rum business, Mr. Pons. Frankly I can't see why the man wanted to get into the Mausoleum, though the materials—the bronze doors and such—are extremely valuable in themselves. I had a theory about the gypsies."

"The gypsies?"

Solar Pons leaned forward with an intent expression on his face that I had often observed when a point of particular importance gained his attention.

"There is an encampment near the village. Or was," the Inspector corrected himself.

"According to my informants they left in the early hours of the morning. They will not get far. They took the Bristol road."

"And yet you have not traced them, Inspector, though over fifteen hours have elapsed? Dear me."

The Inspector's neck turned a dull red.

"It's not as simple as it sounds, Mr. Pons. We have few men. And even a sizeable band can camp undetected in the woods and deserted lanes hereabouts. But we'll find them, never fear."

"And when you have found them, Inspector?"

"Well, Mr. Pons, it's well known that gypsies deal in scrap metal and are not above stealing it. Stokoe was seen at the gypsy camp on at least one occasion by a provision merchant in Penderel Parva who was out delivering with his van. And gypsies are not above using knives on their victims. It is a big wound, it is true, but quite possible."

"I see. Distinctly ingenious, Inspector Morgan. And what do you make of Stokoe's dying words?"

"'The Shaft of Death'? It could have referred to a big knife."

Pons shook his head, looking innocently from the Inspector to Grimpton, who stood awkwardly holding his drink, as though the conversation were beyond him. By contrast, Simmons, the grave-faced butler, was listening eagerly, his face betraying his intense interest.

"I think not, Inspector. Would he not have said, The Blade of Death?"

"The man was dying, Mr. Pons. Who knows what he meant?"

"Well, well. You may be right," said Pons, draining his glass.

"It is getting late, Mr. Grimpton, and our presence here inconveniences you. If we could trouble your chauffeur . . . "

But Inspector Morgan had jumped to his feet, closing his notebook with a snap.

"I have my own car here, Mr. Pons. I will be glad to drive you back to Bath."

"That is settled, then. Goodnight, Mr. Grimpton. We will see you tomorrow."

"I will send the car to the hotel at ten o'clock, Mr. Pons."

"We shall be ready. Come, Parker."

7

It was a dry, bright day the following morning and as we drove out to Penderel Lodge in our host's car Pons was unusually silent, sitting in his corner of the vehicle with his chin sunk upon his chest, his eyes half-closed against the wreathing plumes of blue smoke from his pipe. We had no sooner driven through the lodge-gates before two police-cars followed us in and announced their presence by a blaring of horns.

At a signal from Pons our chauffeur pulled up and we descended. Inspector Morgan's bluff face bore an exultant look as uniformed officers debouched from the police vehicles bearing along with them a dark-haired, sullen figure, roughly dressed, and in handcuffs.

"We have our man, Mr. Pons; their camp was not far," said Inspector Morgan crisply. "It was this gypsy, Mordecai Smith."

"Indeed," said Pons coolly, looking at the manacled figure of the gypsy. "What makes you think that?"

Morgan chuckled.

"Because he has admitted throwing a large knife into the Avon from Pulteney Bridge last night. It will mean dragging the river below the weir but we shall find it, never fear. And in addition I have two witnesses who saw him do it."

"Let us just see what Smith himself says about it," said Pons, going forward to look steadily at the thickset gypsy. He threw his coarse black hair from his eyes and glowered back at Pons unwaveringly.

"I don't know who you are, mister, but I never did it," he said firmly. "I knew Stokoe and it's true we quarrelled. We had enough trouble without convicts joining our camp. I gave him shelter for a few nights and then said he would have to leave."

"Do you deny that you came to blows?" said Inspector Morgan fiercely.

The prisoner turned to face his accuser.

"Aye, that's true too. But I wouldn't kill a man for exchanging a blow or two when provoked."

"Well said, Smith," Solar Pons interjected soothingly. "What do you say to this knife charge?"

"I did throw the knife in the river, sir, but it had nothing to do with Stokoe. One of our band, old Gaffer Jenkins, died three weeks ago and we burned his caravan and all his possessions, as is the Romany custom. But I remembered that some months ago he lent me the knife. It was bad luck to keep it, sir. I couldn't burn it because it was made of metal, handle and all. So I got rid of it by throwing it in the river and that's the truth."

The Inspector had been listening with some impatience.

"A likely story, Mr. Pons. We shall find the knife, I have no doubt, and it will prove to be the murder weapon. It's my opinion Stokoe and Smith went to the Mausoleum to steal bronze and marble from the building but that their quarrel broke out afresh and Smith stabbed him with the knife, which he later threw into the Avon."

"You make it sound convincing, Inspector," said Solar Pons sombrely, studying the prisoner's face. "But I should be disinclined to build your case upon it, if I were you. You have checked the story of the gypsy funeral?"

"It is true, Mr. Pons, that the old man Jenkins died and that his effects were burned in a ceremony at the camp," said Morgan quietly. "I am not denying that."

"Nevertheless, this is an ancient custom of the travellers, Inspector," said Pons. "And the knife might well have belonged to Jenkins. It should be easy enough to prove."

"Have no fear, Mr. Pons. I am certain of my man," said the Inspector briskly, nodding to his officers. "We are going to the Mausoleum now and I expect to get a full confession before the day is out."

"I wish you luck, Inspector," said Solar Pons politely. And he watched the Inspector and his men until both they and their vehicles were out of sight.

"Well, Parker, what do you make of that?"

"Inspector Morgan would appear to have a strong case," I began cautiously. "And things do look black against the gypsy."

Solar Pons chuckled, leading the way back to the Rolls-Royce.

"Tut, Parker, I have trained you better than that. Morgan is building his case on shifting sands. Mark my words, there is something darker and more sinister at the back of this."

"But Smith did know Stokoe," I persisted. "And the two men had quarrelled."

Solar Pons gave me a patient look.

"My dear fellow, I am not denying it. But Morgan is twisting the facts to fit his own theory. That will not do at all. And when he finds that the knife will not match the wound by any conceivable stretch of the imagination, then he will have to start all over again. That is assuming he can even find the knife. The way the river goes rushing over the weir there, it may be anywhere. And in the meantime the good Inspector is wasting valuable hours. I thought better of him, I really did."

He said nothing further until the butler Simmons, had ushered us into the study at Penderel Lodge. It was a big, impressive room, deserted for the moment, with the sunlight spilling in through two handsome French windows at the far end.

"Ah, this will be the scene of the dramatic burglary and chase," said Pons eagerly. He had his pocket lens out now and went up and down quickly. I crossed to a big mahogany desk and stood looking at the serried rows of leather-bound books that marched across the long room, while Pons carried out his examination. He concluded by opening one of the windows and stepping out on to the terrace. He looked sharply about the large expanse of flagstones.

"Well, this would not have given much away," he said as he rejoined me. "The flags are tight-bonded, with no vegetation growing between them. They would not have retained footprints on such a dry night as our client described."

"So what are we left with, Pons?" I asked.

Solar Pons stabbed the air with the stem of his pipe to illustrate his points.

"Enigma upon enigma, my dear Parker. There is no possible

motive at the moment. Until we arrive at that the problem is of formidable opacity."

He allowed himself a wry smile and at that instant the door of the study opened and Septimus Grimpton appeared. He was accompanied by a younger man dressed impeccably in a grey suit with a blue bow-tie. The family resemblance was striking and I was not surprised when our host introduced him as his younger brother, Thaddeus.

The newcomer came forward with a twinkle in his eye and shook hands gravely. He was about sixty and though his thick hair was liberally sprinkled with silver, he exhibited none of the scholarly traits of his brother.

"I live in Bristol and am often here for weekends, Mr. Pons," he explained. "This is a shocking business. I must confess I shall find it fascinating to watch so distinguished a practitioner of the forensic art at work."

Pons made a modest disclaimer and studied the two brothers closely as the master of Penderel Lodge motioned us into comfortable chairs.

"Granger will be joining us in a few moments," he explained. "He has been out for his walk round the estate and is just tidying himself. You and Dr. Parker will stay to lunch, Mr. Pons?"

"With pleasure, Mr. Grimpton. Were you present at the time of the burglaries, Mr. Grimpton?"

This is to our host's brother.

"On one occasion only, to the best of my recollection, Mr. Pons. A nasty affair. Mr. Granger chased an intruder. I'm afraid it was all over by the time I got down."

He chuckled.

"Though judging by the haul it was hardly worth the fellow's while."

"Serious, nevertheless, Thaddeus," said Septimus Grimpton sharply. "And now this man, Stokoe."

"Forgive me, brother," said Thaddeus Grimpton placatingly. "I did not mean to sound frivolous and I realise just how worried you are."

There was something so engagingly old-fashioned about Thaddeus Grimpton and his concern for his older brother that I could not forbear exchanging a brief smile with Pons.

"I am worried about Granger also," Septimus Grimpton confided to us. "His health has been far from good the past few months."

"How so?" said Pons.

He had raised himself in his chair now and his sharp eyes were fixed upon the old man's face.

"Some sort of stomach trouble, Mr. Pons. Granger has had several bouts. But my brother's herbal tea has done him some good, I am glad to say."

Solar Pons shifted his eyes to the younger man. The latter smiled deprecatingly.

"Granger works too hard in my opinion. I fear a stomach ulcer, though the doctor says no. I am a great believer in herbal remedies. I have on several occasions prescribed my own blend of herbal tea for the sufferer."

"I must concur there, Mr. Pons," said Septimus Grimpton. "Thaddeus knows a great deal about the subject. And the tea certainly did Granger good. He was up and about in no time. But I do worry about him. What on earth should I do if he had to leave me because of his health?"

"I am sure it will not come to that, brother. His health seems a good deal better of late."

"That is true, Thaddeus," said our host, somewhat mollified.

"Ah, here is the man himself."

At that moment the door had opened and the wiry, dynamic form of the secretary hurried down the room toward us.

"Apologies, gentlemen. I hope I have not kept you waiting, Mr. Pons?"

"Not at all, Mr. Granger. I have only a few questions."

"In that case we will excuse ourselves," said Septimus Grimpton, rising. "Come, brother."

And the two men, with courteous apologies, glided out and left us alone with the secretary. Granger went to sit down at the desk and looked at us rather defensively, I thought.

"Your employer tells me you have been ill over the past months, Mr. Granger."

"Oh, it is really nothing, Mr. Pons."

"Nevertheless, I should like to hear about it."

"Sickness and vomiting mostly. Followed by stomach cramps. The attacks lasted only a day or two. The doctor tells me nerves, but it was something more definite than that."

"So it would seem, Mr. Granger. But Mr. Grimpton Junior's herbal tea did the trick, I understand."

The secretary laughed, his white teeth gleaming in his face.

"Well, there is certainly something in it, Mr. Pons. On each occasion Mr. Grimpton's beverage put me right within hours."

"Well, that is good to know," said Pons and he did not return to the subject but wandered up and down the study in an apparently aimless fashion. He paused before a long row of dark leather volumes and moving to join him I saw by the gilt titles on their spines that they were account books relating to Penderel Lodge and the estate.

"Where were the keys to the Mausoleum kept, Mr. Granger?"

said Pons, idly turning over the leaves of one of the volumes he had taken down from the shelves.

"In the locked desk here, Mr. Pons. One key is here, as you see. Mr. Grimpton has the other at present."

And he held it up. Pons examined it in desultory fashion and handed it back.

"I must look in at the estate office," he murmured and returned to his examination of the account books.

"A fascinating subject, Parker," he said. "It is a microcosm of English social life itself, the study of a great house over a period of time and has indeed been made the source of a number of outstanding volumes."

"I have no doubt, Pons," said I, "but I fail to see for the moment..."

"As usual, Parker," said Pons somewhat rudely, taking down several of the books from the shelf and running his eyes over them. "Most interesting. Estate accounts. Farm upkeep. Husbandry. Household expenses, even down to the still room. For example, there is an interesting section here devoted to Mr. Grimpton's grandparents and the Mausoleum. Hullo!"

There was such a sharp urgency in his tone that I looked at him in surprise.

"Something has been torn out here."

I moved to his side quickly. I soon saw what he meant; toward the end of the volume in question, about ten pages had been ripped away. Granger was up from the desk now, his face worried.

"I did not know that, Mr. Pons. May I see?"

"By all means."

Pons passed him the volume and the secretary studied it in silence.

"Well, I had never noticed that, though I must confess we do not often consult these old volumes. They were mostly written up by Mr. Grimpton's grandfather and father and they have been discontinued since their time. Perhaps it was done many years ago."

"I think not, Mr. Granger," said Pons sharply. "You will see where the edges of the tear are white. They are comparatively fresh—certainly done within the past year or two—by comparison with the faded and yellowing pages of the main ledger."

"You are certainly correct, Mr. Pons. How peculiar."

The secretary studied the book further, his face still puzzled.

"Do you know to which specific subject the missing section related, Mr. Granger?"

The secretary nodded.

"Nothing of great importance, Mr. Pons. I believe it concerned the construction of the Mausoleum; costs, specifications, time taken; that sort of thing."

"I see."

Solar Pons stood in silence for a moment, his deep-set eyes looking somewhere far beyond me, and there was an awkward pause.

"Well, well, Parker. I think we have seen enough for the moment. A brisk stroll about the grounds would not come amiss. Thank you, Mr. Granger. You have been most helpful. We will see you at lunch."

And he led the way from the room.

✑ 8

We walked swiftly down the terrace and away from the house. Pons was going so fast that I had a job to keep up.

"Where are we going, Pons?"

"To the estate office, Parker. I have a fancy to see where that third key is kept. And, if there is time before lunch, I should like to put a few questions to Hoskins, the gardener."

As he spoke we rounded the corner of the house and there, spread before us across the rolling parkland bathed in the November sunshine, were the substantial outlines of extensive farm buildings emerging from beyond a belt of trees. But before that a massive glasshouse rose on the banks of an ornamental lake. The squeak of a heavily-laden wheelbarrow became apparent to the ear and Pons quickened his steps.

"Ah, Parker, if I mistake not, here is the man himself."

Hoskins turned out to be a middle-aged, stolid sort of person with a fringe of greying whiskers which gave his face a nineteenth century aspect. He rested his barrow-load of red and gold leaves and looked at Pons somewhat defensively, I thought.

"Mr. Pons, is it? Mr. Grimpton's guest? Well, gentlemen, I must be civil seeing as how you're staying at the Lodge but I've been plagued a deal by the police since yesterday, I can tell you."

"That's as may be, Hoskins, but I will not detain you long. And I have nothing to do with the official force."

The gardener looked relieved and squared his shoulders as though Pons were about to take him on at a round or two of boxing.

"Fire away, sir."

"It is just that I have a fancy to know a little more of this man Stokoe's wound."

Hoskins' face clouded over.

"Ah, sir, it was a terrible gash. Several inches long, almost over the heart. A miracle the poor man was still alive. Blood everywhere."

Solar Pons narrowed his eyes and stabbed with the stem of his pipe to emphasise his points.

"You are a man, Hoskins, who is used to inflicting wounds with various weapons."

"Eigh, sir?"

Hoskins looked startled and stepped back a little warily.

"In a manner of speaking of course. You wound the earth with a variety of instruments; the spade, the fork, the pick, the mattock and so on."

The gardener's face cleared.

"Yes, sir. I take your meaning."

"And you are therefore familiar with the type of shape made by the various tools you use."

"I should hope so, sir."

Pons nodded with satisfaction.

"What type of wound was inflicted on the unfortunate Mr. Stokoe?"

"Large, made by something big and heavy, sir. And with considerable weight, I would have thought. Like the digging blade of a pick-axe."

Solar Pons' face was alive with interest as he stared at the gardener.

"Thank you, Hoskins. I find that most interesting. You are certain the wound could not have been inflicted with a knife?"

The gardener snorted with disgust and shook his head.

"Certainly not, sir. And no one who really knows anything about such things could mistake it."

"Not even a large knife?"

Hoskins shook his head even more emphatically.

"By no means, sir. The wound was far too big. There was a huge piece of flesh scooped right out of his chest. I know, sir, because I pulled his shirt back to have a look."

"Inspector Morgan seems to think it was a knife."

"With all respect, sir, the Inspector is wrong."

Pons replaced his pipe in his mouth and puffed at it with considerable satisfaction, it seemed to me.

"I just wanted to be sure, Hoskins. You have been most helpful. I have only one more question. Was Stokoe going toward the house when you found him or away from it?"

"Toward the house, sir. I am positive."

"He could not have simply spun around in falling?"

Again the gardener shook his head.

"By no means, sir. He was trying to drag himself across the grass as I went to restrain him. He kept muttering about 'The Shaft of Death'. It made no sense to me, sir."

"Nor anyone else for the moment. Thank you again, Hoskins. Here is a pound for your trouble. No doubt you can put it to good use at your local hostelry."

The gardener's face brightened and he took the note with alacrity, transferring it quickly to the pocket of his corduroy trousers.

"Good day to you, gentlemen. And if there's anything further you require to know, I'm usually to be found on this side of the house."

There was a smile on his face as Pons resumed his walk and I kept at his side, refraining from asking any questions as I could see that his agile mind was revolving a number of possibilities. Five minutes more took us to a mellow brick stable block, on top of which a cupola was set, the sunshine winking back from the gilt hands of a clock which now indicated the midday hour.

A groom in riding clothes was forking straw in a corner of the stable yard and readily pointed out the estate office, a comfortably appointed chamber, obviously part of the estate manager's private house. Pons rapped on the glass-panelled door but there was obviously no one there so after a momentary hesitation he pushed open the door and we walked in.

A large mahogany desk; several shelves of books and box-files of farm accounts; a swivel chair; and two filing cabinets almost filled the interior. A beaker of hot coffee stood upon the desk surface, steam still rising from it, so it was obvious the occupant had stepped out for only a few moments.

A decent thick-pile rug covered half the parquet floor and a cheerful fire burned in the brick fireplace, before which a red setter was languidly sprawled. It took no notice of our entrance, except to regard us with a liquid eye, and then dropped back again, apparently satisfied, to its motionless contemplation of the flames.

We had been standing there for perhaps ten or fifteen seconds when the door which obviously led to the house beyond was flung violently open and a huge, red-faced man with a yellow moustache, dressed in a hairy tweed jacket and riding breeches, glowered at us.

"No trespassing allowed," he said crisply. "I shall oblige you to state your business."

"If you will have the kindness to introduce yourself we shall do the same," said Pons imperturbably.

The military gentleman's puce expression deepened.

"I know who I am," he grunted. "Captain Mannering. Estate manager. Who are you?"

"Solar Pons. This is my friend and colleague, Dr. Lyndon Parker. We are the house-guests of Mr. Grimpton."

"Indeed."

Mannering stared at us in an offensive manner and then sat down at the desk in front of his beaker of coffee. He did not ask us to sit but continued frowning at the wall in front of him.

"I am investigating the murder of the man Stokoe," said Solar Pons. "I should like a glimpse of the key of the Mausoleum which I understand is kept in this office."

Pons' request had an electrifying effect on the Captain. He went white, swallowed once or twice and his face gradually assumed a mottled aspect.

"As if the police were not enough," he muttered under his breath.

Then he turned his head to glare with bloodshot blue eyes at my companion.

"Who are you to question me?" he demanded. "You are not a police officer. Of what concern is it to you?"

"Nevertheless, I should like to see that key," Pons went on imperturbably.

The Captain's hand crashed down on to the surface of the desk with a vehemence which made the coffee beaker jump and slop half its contents on to the blotter. The Captain rose to his feet. Pons was a tall man but this formidable figure seemed to tower over him.

"I must warn you, Mr. Pons. Don't meddle in my affairs."

There was a mocking smile on Solar Pons' lips as he stared steadily at the other; in the end it was the Captain who lowered his eyes.

"You are being extremely foolish, Captain Mannering," Pons said quietly. "However, it makes no matter. You are only postponing the inevitable. Come, Parker."

We left the figure of the Captain standing at the desk as though turned to stone. Once across the stable yard Pons burst into a short laugh.

"Well, Parker, what do you think of our Captain Mannering?"

"What a rude brute, Pons," I said hotly. "His behaviour is extremely suspicious."

"Is it not, Parker."

"When I tell Grimpton how he has behaved he will make him give up the key," I said.

Solar Pons put his hand on my arm.

"No, no, my dear fellow, it will not do. We must not alarm him."

"But the key is vital, Pons. He must be made to give it up."

"If he has it, Parker," said Solar Pons enigmatically.

"Eigh, Pons?"

I stared at my companion in irritation.

"The Captain strikes me as an extremely frightened man, Parker. Just let me have your thoughts upon this little problem."

"It gets darker and deeper, Pons," I said.

"Does it not? But just apply those latent ratiocinative gifts I have so assiduously tried to cultivate."

"We have a murder and no discernible motive."

"Capital, Parker!"

Solar Pons' eyes were sparkling.

"We have a mention of a 'Shaft of Death' which clouds the issue still further."

"Pray continue."

"A massive wound, no weapon, and a knife which Inspector Morgan insists is the murder instrument and yet which cannot possibly fit, if all the facts are correct."

"You continue to sparkle, Parker. You are showing an amazing grasp of the problems."

"A gypsy who has a possible motive for the crime, swears he is innocent. The secretary is somewhat reticent, it seems to me."

"Ah, you have noticed that, have you?"

"Captain Mannering is acting in a highly suspicious manner. As estate manager he is familiar with the Mausoleum. The specifications of that building are missing from Grimpton's study. Even the gardener, Hoskins, does not believe a knife inflicted Stokoe's wound."

I stopped and stared with disbelief at Pons' widening smile.

"Good heavens, Pons. Hoskins is a strong and powerful man. As you yourself said, he knows how to wield heavy tools. You cannot mean it! Even Hoskins himself admitted that the blow which felled Stokoe could have been dealt with the obverse side of a pickaxe!"

"Could it not, Parker. You have admirably summed up some of the slight difficulties which beset one of the most interesting problems which has ever come my way. But here we are at the house again. Our little walk has quite given me an appetite for lunch."

9

The afternoon passed quietly. Pons was absent for a while, and I heard him talking with Granger the secretary. I took a short walk about the grounds after lunch and observed the gardener in the distance. I kept an eye on him but despite my efforts at remaining under cover he soon spotted me and retreated into the glasshouse by the lake with a highly suspicious air, it seemed to me.

I took a circular route that brought me within viewing distance of the main gates and, attracted by the noise of engines, noted the two police vehicles, no doubt containing Inspector Morgan and his sullen gypsy prisoner. To my surprise, instead of coming toward the house, the vehicles disappeared through the entrance of the estate and shortly afterward the hum of their motors died in the distance.

I continued my walk with many questions occupying my mind and on my return to the house found Septimus Grimpton and Pons walking up and down the terrace. As I hesitated Pons caught sight of me.

"Don't go, my dear fellow. Mr. Grimpton and I are merely discussing a few details of the estate."

The old scholar shook his head, his fringe of white hair whipped about by the rising wind.

"This is a baffling business, Mr. Pons. I don't know what I should have done without you being here. We might all be murdered in our beds."

Pons smiled gently.

"I hardly think so, Mr. Grimpton. I submit it is more a case of old friends falling out."

Grimpton shook his head.

"The servants are terrified, though they keep up appearances well before guests. My brother has been a great settling influence but even Simmons seems affected by the old stories about my grandfather."

"The butler?"

Pons' face expressed keen interest as he turned toward our host in the pale November sunshine.

"That is correct, Mr. Pons. The old chap has been with the family a good many years. I could see he was bursting to tell you the story when we were all in the study with the Inspector."

"You intrigue me, Mr. Grimpton. Just what stories are these?"

"Fairy-tales, Mr. Pons. Legends that have been linked with every vagabond and itinerant traveller seen about the place."

"Nevertheless, I shall have to ask you to be more precise, Mr. Grimpton."

The old man's face looked worried but his voice was steady enough as he turned to face my companion.

"You must remember that my grandfather was an immensely wealthy man, Mr. Pons. And stories and superstition accrete round such wealth. It was reputed that he amassed a great fortune in cash, plate and precious stones. This was supposed to have been hidden somewhere in the house and grounds. It was referred to in the village, I believe, somewhat picturesquely as 'The Treasure of Brimstone Grimpton'. Arrant nonsense, of course. I doubt whether there was ever such a thing. But my poor father wasted a great deal of time searching for it."

"Nevertheless, it is intriguing, Mr. Grimpton. I take it your father never found anything?"

Grimpton shook his head.

"Not that I ever heard, Mr. Pons."

He chuckled.

"It certainly never descended to me or I should be a great deal richer and should not have to worry so much about Mannering and the running of the estate."

"I should not speak of this again, Mr. Grimpton. It does not do to let rumour fly and if the legend were to become attached to the violent death of the man Stokoe, the resulting notoriety..."

"Good heavens, Mr. Pons! I had not thought of that."

Grimpton's face looked shocked and his mouth sagged open. Solar Pons took him by the arm.

"You mentioned something about Captain Mannering?"

Grimpton's features looked even more lugubrious.

"He has a drink problem, I fear. Yet I would hate to discharge him. He has given sterling service to the estate over the years."

"That is indeed a difficulty, Mr. Grimpton. And one that you alone can solve. In the meantime Parker and I have problems enough of our own. I am sure you will excuse us, Mr. Grimpton. Come, Parker."

During the latter part of the afternoon Pons was again closeted with Granger the secretary and then took the opportunity to visit the upper floor of the rambling house. When he descended he drew me to one side in his usual brisk manner.

"Now, Parker, I require assistance. I would like you to engage Simmons in a little conversation. I have a mind to delve into the mysteries of his pantry."

"Eigh, Pons?"

Solar Pons shook his head, a whimsical smile on his face.

"This is your chance to shine, Parker. Here comes the man now."

"But what shall I talk about, Pons?"

"Anything that comes to mind, my dear fellow. The weather, politics, the decay of the country estate—I am sure you will think of something."

And with that he darted off down the corridor, leaving me to face the grave-featured old man who bore down upon me with a tray in his hand. In the event I think I acquitted myself creditably, for I chose the one subject the butler had a passion for. He had strange and very strong preconceived ideas about the cultivation and serving of exotic fruit raised under glass and his strictures upon the unfortunate gardener Hoskins and his ministrations in the glasshouse were quite severe.

He was well into his stride on the best way to raise peaches when Pons reappeared, an enigmatic smile on his face, dusting his elbows. He nodded pleasantly at the old man and I excused myself to join him.

"Well done, Parker, you have excelled yourself. You are quite a horticulturist, I see."

"What were you doing in the butler's pantry, Pons?"

"Observing, Parker. And drawing conclusions. There are quite enough materials in there to make up a strong emetic mixture, ranging from curries and chutneys to the most virulent and exotic forms of spices from our great Indian Empire."

"Indeed, Pons," I ventured mildly. "But I fail to follow you."

"It is not the first time, Parker," said Pons, a twinkle in his eye. "But we have been asked to stay on to dinner this evening. I have but a few more questions to ask before coming to some definite conclusions."

And he said nothing further until dinner, breaking silence only at the coffee and dessert stage. Instead, he had listened with rapt attention to the conversation between the two Grimpton brothers and Granger the secretary; the talk was mostly of a trivial nature, about the great house and its occupants, the state of the Home Farm and the general running of the estate but Pons seemed to find it of inordinate interest.

At length there was a lull and Septimus Grimpton profited by the short silence to ask after the secretary's health.

"It is a great deal better, sir, thank you," Granger returned. He looked searchingly at his employer, as though he feared there might be an ulterior motive behind the question. Thaddeus Grimpton beamed jovially behind his glasses and once again I was touched by the obvious affinity which existed between these two so different brothers.

"Your brother's herbal tea seems to have done the trick

perfectly, Mr. Grimpton," Solar Pons observed, giving the secretary a reassuring smile.

"Thaddeus is a kind fellow," said the elder Grimpton warmly. "He does a deal of good in Bristol and elsewhere too. He is on the board of several charitable trusts; a prison visitor; active on the hospital board . . ."

An electrifying change had come over Solar Pons and he gave Septimus Grimpton a hawk-like glance from his piercing eyes.

"Indeed, Mr. Grimpton. Well, Parker and I have much to do. We must be going. There is a concert at the Theatre Royal tomorrow and, I understand, an excellent Roman exhibition at the Guildhall."

"Really, Mr. Pons, I do not quite follow," said our host, bewilderment written on his features.

"It means that your little problem is solved, Mr. Grimpton. I quite forgot to tell you. Inspector Morgan made an arrest this morning. One of the band of gypsies. He killed Stokoe with an extra large knife, which he later threw into the Avon. I do not think you will be troubled further."

"You astonish me, Mr. Pons."

Our host was on his feet too as Pons rose swiftly.

"Extraordinary, Pons," I began when my companion gave me a warning glance.

"I am sorry to have imposed upon your hospitality, Mr. Grimpton, but as you can see Inspector Morgan was quite capable after all and had the correct solution."

"I still do not understand, Mr. Pons."

The entire dinner party had risen now and my own bewilderment was re-echoed on the faces of the younger Grimpton and the secretary.

"But what was the motive, Mr. Pons?"

"Theft and robbery, Mr. Grimpton. Nothing but a common quarrel among petty thieves. The case is closed. Allow me to congratulate you on the resumption of calm at Penderel Lodge and to take my leave in order that Parker and I may resume our interrupted holiday."

"You disappoint me, Mr. Pons."

There was sadness in our host's voice and I glanced swiftly at Pons but he only answered blandly.

"Disappointment comes to us all at times, Mr. Grimpton, and I too am sorry that I was unable to display those modest gifts which you so flatteringly believe me to possess. Now I really must say goodnight. No, we shall not need the car. It is a beautiful evening and I fancy a brisk walk back to Bath."

A few moments later we were out of the house and striding across the park in the moonlight, the winding road before us. I had a job to keep up with my companion who walked furiously, as though possessed by some galvanic force.

"What on earth are you at, Pons?" I spluttered when I at last caught up with him.

"Let us hurry, Parker. We have not a moment to lose. I fancy our man will strike again tonight when he fancies the coast is clear. I want to be in position long before that moment comes."

I stared at Pons in amazement.

"I do not follow you, Pons."

"My dear fellow," said Solar Pons, unable to keep the note of weariness from his voice. "What on earth do you think that display was for at dinner just now? To allay our man's suspicions. Now he knows that both the police and Solar Pons are off the case he will make another attempt to achieve his objective."

"Then we are not going back to Bath? The case is not closed?"

"Tut, Parker. You disappoint me. Just save your breath for we have a stiff walk before us. I want to get in position near the Mausoleum long before our man appears. The game's afoot!"

And he said no more but plunged along the winding estate road, all powdered silver in the moonlight, at such a rate that I was breathless long before we reached the lodge-entrance.

10

Pons unhesitatingly swung through the main gates of Penderel Lodge and turned left on to the main road back toward the village of Penderel Parva. He put his finger alongside his nose to enjoin caution.

"We must be seen to be well clear of the estate, Parker. That is why we must hurry."

"But where are we going, Pons?"

Solar Pons gave a brief chuckle.

"Farther down the estate boundary, Parker. I understand there are a number of gaps in the walls and hedges. It may take us some while to work back up to the Mausoleum. These woods will be dark, despite the moonlight."

He consulted his watch.

"I estimate that he will not make his move for another hour, until the household is abed. It will then take him at least twenty minutes on foot to reach the Mausoleum. We have already been twenty minutes on the road. That should leave us another hour or so to work our way back."

The way indeed seemed interminable. The moon was high now and shed a brilliant light on road and hedgerow. I was a little perturbed at this but we met nothing on the way and, just before we reached the outskirts of Penderel Parva, Pons led me down a small side-turning which followed the estate wall as it curved away into the middle distance.

"Silence here, Parker," he whispered. "I fancy this is Grimpton's private road and I have no wish to be disturbed by any of his inquisitive cottagers."

We pushed our way along in the shadow of the trees and presently came to a place where the wall fell away and was replaced by a high spile fence. We followed it for another two hundred yards and eventually found a spot where the staves were distorted with damp, leaving us enough space to squeeze through. Our feet shuffled eerily among the fallen leaves as we walked through the dark belts of woodland, guiding ourselves by the faint moonlight which filtered through the bare branches.

The way was longer than we had thought and several times Pons halted and carefully orientated himself. After a stiff uphill walk, which I estimated as taking about twenty minutes, we came out of a silent ride in the forest and on to a cart-track which wound away through the trees. It went in the right direction and with the easier going it was only a few minutes more before we found it joined the tarmacadam estate road about a quarter of a mile from the lodge-gates.

"Just over here, Parker," Pons whispered, his lean face alive with suppressed excitement. "And not a word if you please."

I followed him off the road and into another belt of trees and a short while later we skirted a fringe of bushes to find ourselves in front of a wide expanse of roadway, the white blanched expanse of the Mausoleum standing up sharp and clear before us. Pons moved over and knelt behind a fallen tree-trunk, where I joined him. He put his mouth up against my ear.

"It wants but a few minutes to midnight, Parker. I think we are just in time."

Indeed, we had not been there more than a quarter of an hour before his keen ears picked out a hurried step on the roadway. Then it stopped and there was a long period of silence. Again Pons bent to me.

"He has left the road and gone on to the grass, Parker. He should be here in a minute or so."

His grip tightened on my arm and a few moments later I saw what his keen sight had already picked out; a tall, sturdy figure, heavily muffled in a thick overcoat, which glided cautiously from under the trees. I felt my breath catch in my throat, as there was something inexpressibly sinister about the black shape in the whiteness of the moonlight at that dead hour of the night.

The figure looked round sharply as it crossed from under the trees and then went swiftly up the steps to the great bronze door of the Mausoleum. A moment later I heard the harsh grating of the key in the lock and the gap where the door had been showed black against the white façade. There was another long silence and then I caught the beam of a torch from within the interior. Solar Pons rose to his feet.

"Come, Parker. Our man will be too distracted. There will never be a better opportunity."

We quickly crossed the concourse, bright with moonlight, taking care to make as little noise as possible. We gained the steps without incident and had got up quite close to the doors when there came a harsh grating noise from within the Mausoleum, which set my teeth on edge. Pons swiftly flattened himself to one side of the door and I joined him within the shadow of the buttress. Pons' face expressed satisfaction.

"I have been extremely lax in this matter, Parker. The groove in the floor should have told me. Well, there is nothing better than having one's theories tested in practice. I think we may venture in safely without disturbing our quarry."

He glided into the blackness of the interior and without hesitation I followed. I shall never forget the sight which met our eyes. The interior of the Mausoleum was dimly lit by the rays of an electric lantern whose light was flung upwards from an oblong slit in the floor of the building.

The first thing which struck my eye was the monstrous, elongated shadow of a human being on the domed ceiling. My nerves jumped and I clutched at Pons instinctively. A moment later I saw that the white, dead face which stared back at me from the top of the sarcophagus was indeed marble and belonged to the tomb of our client's grandmother.

The entire structure had been pivoted round on its base which ran in a circular groove which I had originally thought to be an incised pattern in the flooring.

"The bloodied hand-marks on the sarcophagus, Pons!" I whispered excitedly.

Pons nodded grimly and motioned me to silence. We moved forward quietly and as we drew nearer I could see that a shallow flight of steps led downward into the aperture that the removal of the sarcophagus had disclosed. We had silently covered half the distance when there was a sharp whirring noise from below, followed immediately by a soft thud and one of the most terrible cries it has ever been my misfortune to hear uttered by a human throat.

I stood paralysed as that unearthly scream echoed and re-echoed round the dome of the Mausoleum but Pons dashed forward, all caution abandoned. I could hear his feet echoing over the steps as I hurried down after him. The cry had ceased now and a moment later I learned the reason why. Pons was kneeling by the crumpled figure at the foot of the steps, while scarlet pumped steadily over the stone floor.

The electric lantern set to shine upon the stout wooden door that barred the passage disclosed a terrible and bizarre sight. From the ceiling protruded a shining metal shaft which had descended with tremendous force from a slot in the wall. The metal arm ended in a lead-cased weight into the tip of which was set the broad blade of an enormous knife, now coated with blood and rust.

"'The Shaft of Death'!" said Pons, white-faced. "I did not know it would end like this. Your department, I think, Parker. But be careful, in case there are any other lethal devices left by old Brimstone Grimpton."

I bent over the recumbent figure in the expensive overcoat only to recoil with a cry of shocked surprise. It was not just the terrible, gaping wound in the chest, so tremendous that it actually exposed the heart; or the certainty that a corpse lay before me in the passage; or even the horribly distorted face, the staring eyes or the tongue protruding from the bleeding lips. It was an abysmal catalogue all too familiar to me as a medical practitioner.

I gently laid the mutilated remains back on the floor and stared in silence at the dreadfully changed face of Thaddeus Grimpton.

"Did you know this, Pons?"

Solar Pons stood and gave me an enigmatic glance.

"It came to me rather late, Parker, I regret to say. But we have other work before us. This diabolical toy appears to be actuated by a spring concealed beneath the flagstone here."

He bent to demonstrate and with a sudden whirring of gears, which made us start back in alarm, the dreadful weapon withdrew silently to its former position between two stones in the wall where it was difficult to detect. Pons had knelt again and was busy about Grimpton s clothing. He drew forth a bundle of blood-stained documents.

"The missing estate material, Pons."

Solar Pons nodded.

"Containing, I have no doubt, the specifications and details of the building of this passage beneath the sarcophagus, Parker. Though it is obvious the old man said nothing in there about his deadly sentinel."

"But what is the point of all this, Pons?"

"The object of the game, my dear fellow. Which lies behind that door. Just have a care and stand back."

Carefully skirting the flagstone set directly in front of the door, Pons cautiously tried the bronze handle. He gently opened the door and shone the lantern's beam within the small chamber disclosed. The light danced upon paintings stacked against the dusty walls; velvet-lined cases, some half-open, disclosing silverware; leather bags stacked in profusion upon a heavy table. I entered behind Pons as the lantern disclosed yet more valuables. Pons hefted one of the bags thoughtfully. The rotted fastening split and a cascade of sovereigns rained upon the table.

"Heavens, Pons!" I said in a none too steady voice. "The Treasure of old Brimstone Grimpton!!!!"

"For once the legends did not lie, Parker," said Pons softly. "There will be little sleep for us tonight. We must first apprise my client of his sad loss and then telephone Inspector Morgan."

He pulled reflectively at the lobe of his ear, the lantern beam dancing golden on the coins which had already cost two men's lives and had endangered that of a third.

"The gypsy must be released at once, Parker. Let us put matters in train without delay."

"I do not know how to thank you, Mr. Pons. Though I cannot tell you what a shock it was to learn of my brother's treacherous behaviour."

Solar Pons looked sympathetically at Septimus Grimpton, who sat the other side of the library table from us, the sunlight from the windows making a halo round his white locks and revealing the ravages that the last three days had wrought upon him. Inspector Morgan sat awkwardly twisting a pencil between his fingers opposite, while Granger, the secretary, made the fifth member of our party.

"It was a long-planned strategy, I am afraid, Mr. Grimpton. My own inquiries since and Inspector Morgan's investigations in Bristol have revealed your brother's intense jealousy over your inheriting this house and estate."

"But he was well provided for in my father's will, Mr. Pons."

Solar Pons shook his head.

"The traditional jealousy of the younger son, I am afraid, Mr. Grimpton. Though I was incredibly obtuse on this occasion, until a very late stage."

"Come, Pons," I protested. "It was a brilliant performance, particularly as there was no discernible motive."

"I am still completely in the dark, Mr. Pons," said the secretary. "Why, for example, should Mr. Grimpton's brother make these crude burglary attempts?"

Solar Pons tented his fingers before him and looked sombrely round the table.

"Desperation, Mr. Granger. For years he had been searching for the money and valuables recovered from the chamber below the Mausoleum. He regarded them as his own portion of his patrimony, despite the generous provision made in his father's will. He was convinced there was a hiding place and that some record would be found among the estate papers. That was why he cultivated you so assiduously during the past years, Mr. Grimpton."

"He was here a good deal at weekends, from Bristol, Mr. Pons."

Solar Pons nodded.

"Exactly. And one could imagine his annoyance when he discovered a year ago that you had engaged a secretary to help you with your scholarly researches."

"How so, Mr. Pons?"

"Because he was in the habit of spending long periods in the library. I have that from your butler, Simmons. He was undoubtedly searching for clues. But when Mr. Granger came things changed drastically. The library was no longer available to him. Or, if it were, he could not very well rummage through the shelves and document files without engendering suspicion in the breast of Mr. Granger here."

I stared at Pons for a long moment.

"So he staged the burglaries, Pons?"

"Not quite, Parker. He had to ensure at times that Mr. Granger was out of the way and nowhere near the library. An illness of some sort provided the answer."

"But Mr. Grimpton's herbal tea did me the world of good, Mr. Pons," the secretary protested.

Solar Pons gave a thin smile.

"By clearing up a stomach disorder that Grimpton had himself induced. I found a large assortment of highly potent but quite harmless substances in Simmons' pantry. To an amateur herbalist like Grimpton it would not take much to concoct a mixture that would upset the most stable stomach. It could be introduced into food or drink in a number of ways. And Simmons has told me that small quantities of things like spices and curry powders have been missing over a long period."

"I am sorry to speak ill of your brother, Mr. Grimpton," said the secretary bitterly. "But that is a most damnable thing."

"I am not excusing my brother, Granger," said Septimus Grimpton in a low voice. "He appears to have been the blackest of villains."

"Masquerading in the guise of a person of great charity and compassion," put in Inspector Morgan. "I am afraid I was completely on the wrong track over the gypsy, Mr. Pons."

"It was an understandable error, Inspector. And fitted most of the known facts at the time. This was the confused background which suited our man. With Mr. Granger out of the way he could pursue his search uninterrupted."

"But the burglaries, Pons," I interrupted.

"That was elementary, Parker. They were the most palpable simulations, staged merely to hide the real purpose of the search. On one occasion Mr. Grimpton here surprised his brother late at night in the study; on another Mr. Granger chased an intruder. Thaddeus Grimpton, when disturbed, had little time other than to hastily seize a few items from the house and make his escape through the French windows, leaving the occupants to believe a burglar responsible. As you know, we have found the things in a trunk in his room. I have no doubt he conveniently reappeared at the height of the disturbances and, of course, the burglaries would have occurred only when he was staying here. I noted that from our conversations, gentlemen."

Septimus Grimpton passed a shaky hand across his brow.

"That is perfectly correct, Mr. Pons. I had not seen the connection."

"There is no reason why you should have, Mr. Grimpton. And you would certainly not have suspected your own brother of any ill will."

"If I had known of his intentions, Mr. Pons, I would gladly have shared my grandfather's treasure with him."

Solar Pons smiled wryly.

"Ah, there we have one of the supreme ironies of life, Mr. Grimpton. Two men lying dead and all these tragic circumstances, with greed again responsible. Now, from what Inspector Morgan tells me and from what I have been able to piece together, it is almost certain that the man Stokoe and your brother together plotted to steal the secret cache of valuables from the Mausoleum. Your grandfather's eccentricity had devised, as he thought, a perfect way of guarding his valuables. He had constructed the secret room beneath the sarcophagus of his wife, telling everyone at the time that he himself would be interred there. This was the reason the plinth pivoted on that curious turn-table. I had seen the circular groove in the floor when we visited the building but foolishly failed to make the connection, taking it to be part of the pattern of the tiling. It was cunningly done, so there may be some slight mitigation in my own defence.

"Of course, it was obvious to me at once that the quarrel and the knife theory regarding the gypsy would not hold water. It was evident from the circumstances that the fatal blow had been struck within the Mausoleum. But there was the problem of the missing weapon; and furthermore, there was no trace within the chamber of the man who had struck the blow. I saw these facts at once and also noted the curious corollary that the old gentleman himself was interred on the far side of the Mausoleum, away from his wife. But I had not then learned of the story of the treasure from Mr. Grimpton, neither did anyone know anything about the hidden chamber, so that I was unable at that time to piece these disparate segments together."

"Come, Pons," I said. "You are being too modest."

Solar Pons made a faint clicking noise with his tongue.

"I should have seen the connection at once, Parker. The fact that the grandfather was interred on the far side should have plainly spelled it out to me. He left careful instructions in his will about that, I now understand. And to guard the valuables he left the terrible device, so picturesquely referred to by the unfortunate Stokoe as 'The Shaft of Death'. Perhaps you can enlighten us there, Mr. Grimpton?"

"I cannot vouch for it, Mr. Pons, but I often heard my father say that Grandfather was a wonderful mechanic and watch-maker. It was a particular hobby of his."

Solar Pons inclined his head with a sombre expression.

"He said nothing, of course, about this diabolical instrument in his estate book notes, so your brother would have had no inkling of the danger. And he naturally did not anticipate Stokoe's own treachery in attempting to secure the money for himself."

"I am still not clear about all this, Pons," I said.

"And yet it was all there before us, Parker," said Solar Pons. "I myself failed to draw the necessary conclusions until quite late in the day. The bloodied hand-prints Stokoe left on the tomb effigy were not simply put there when he tried to steady himself when dying. Gravely wounded as he was, his first instinct was to protect the secret by pushing the plinth back over the entrance passage. In so doing he used almost his last strength and he was undoubtedly on his way to the house either to warn or upbraid your brother when he collapsed and died, Mr. Grimpton."

The old man shook his head.

"A terrible story, Mr. Pons."

"The connection between Stokoe and the late Thaddeus Grimpton is by no means clear," said Inspector Morgan, clearing his throat.

"Yet, it was perfectly simple once we had learned the motive," said Pons. "Grimpton had the secret and he guessed, rightly, that a fortune lay within his grasp. But to remove the treasure he needed a man more used to danger and the sterner side of life. He was himself a scholar and a man well into late middle-age. He required a ruthless, younger man, who would work under his direction for a share of the fortune. He found that man in the person of the ex-convict, Abel Stokoe."

"I see, Pons," I said. "You mean...?"

"Exactly, Parker," Solar Pons interrupted cuttingly. "It leapt at me when Mr. Grimpton here said his brother was a member of charitable trusts and a prison visitor. Bristol Gaol was the former habitation of Stokoe, and Grimpton visited there. He no doubt cultivated Stokoe over several years and primed and recruited him before his release. He would have been the perfect tool. Used to dangerous house-breaking work at night and physically strong, as he would need to be, to remove the materials Grimpton hoped to find in the vault. But the two men either quarrelled or else Stokoe decided, unknown to his employer, to make his own attempt on the Mausoleum.

"The doors had been greased so as to avoid attracting attention by making a noise at dead of night and Grimpton had stolen the key from Captain Mannering's desk at the estate office, after having found it impossible to get at either of the two keys Mr. Granger kept in the study."

They were always under lock and key, Mr. Pons," said the secretary earnestly. "I made sure of that."

"So that was what you meant at the Home Farm, Pons," I said. "But how did Stokoe get the key?"

"By surreptitiously making a wax impression of the stolen one," said Pons. "We can be reasonably sure that this would have been done when the two men first visited the Mausoleum to try to uncover its secret. They may well have made several nocturnal excursions for, as you have seen, Inspector, the catch which actuates the pivot is damnably hard to find."

"That is so, Mr. Pons."

"You may remember, Parker, I particularly questioned Mr. Granger about the keys and was reasonably satisfied that no one could have had access to them. There remained then the only other known key, that at the Estate Office. When we visited Captain Mannering there, I saw at once that the key must be missing. He was so ill at ease and inclined to bluster that I was sure the key left in his charge had been stolen. He felt guilty and realised he might be implicated after the Mausoleum had been found open and Stokoe murdered. He was not going to admit to the key's loss without a struggle and nor do I blame him."

"Even so, Mr. Pons..." our host began.

"What you decide about your Estate Manager is your business, Mr. Grimpton," continued Pons. "I am merely stating the facts."

"But how would anyone have got the key?" I asked.

"Pshaw, Parker, use the evidence of your eyes. We were complete strangers when we arrived at Home Farm yet the groom immediately directed us to the Estate Office, which was empty. Any intruder would have only to search the desk undisturbed to find the key. And as Mr. Thaddeus Grimpton was a trusted member of the household and might well have visited the Farm in the normal course of events, nothing would have been easier than to get hold of that key. I do not like telling tales out of school, Mr. Grimpton, but it was common knowledge that the Captain liked the bottle and he might not have discovered the theft of the key for weeks. He only realised its significance following the tragic events at the Mausoleum and quite naturally attempted to cover things up when I so unexpectedly visited him."

"You make it sound so easy, Pons," I said.

Solar Pons shook his head.

"On the contrary, Parker, I have been extraordinarily obtuse. It is extremely difficult when working without discernible motive, as we were. And the gypsy Smith's action in throwing the knife into the river confused the issue."

"Do not remind me of that, Mr. Pons," said Inspector Morgan ruefully.

"You acted perfectly correctly as an official representative of the law, Inspector. Stokoe had stayed at the caravans with Smith and his fellow gypsies. For the business he had on hand in the neighbourhood, it probably suited his purpose to submerge himself among the Romanies. And if anything had gone wrong they might well have been blamed. But he was a surly fellow, as we have learned, and he quarrelled with his gypsy hosts and was told to leave. This was awkward, as he was placed close to his base of operations at the estate. He could not stay at Penderel

Parva because it was too small and might excite comment so he took cheap lodgings in Bath. There Inspector Morgan recovered the mould from which he made the fourth key to the Mausoleum entrance, the one found in the door. You have been extremely useful in that direction, Inspector."

"It is good of you to say so, Mr. Pons," the Inspector murmured. "Though I was so taken up with the gypsy and the knife theory that I quite overlooked a number of salient points."

"Most understandable," said Solar Pons soothingly. "It was your gardener, Hoskins, who inadvertently gave me a vital clue, Mr. Grimpton."

Our host looked up with quick interest.

"What was that, Mr. Pons?"

"We spoke of spades and mattocks and such broad-bladed instruments. I saw at once that such a weapon would have perfectly fitted Stokoe's terrible wound and that again directed my attention back to the Mausoleum and the dying man's cryptic reference to 'The Shaft of Death'."

Pons turned to the table and picked up his pipe with a frown.

"When we recovered Mordecai Smith's knife from the Avon I saw it was a hopeless match and had to let him go," said the Inspector resignedly.

"And that, I think, Parker, almost clears up the salient features of one of the strangest and most terrible cases in which I have ever been involved."

"There remains one important point, Pons," I said mischievously.

Solar Pons paused in lighting his pipe, his brown corrugated.

"And what might that be?"

"I am sure Mr. Granger will forgive me, but I suspected him at one stage. He had every opportunity of finding the Mausoleum details from the records and of staging the sham burglaries."

Solar Pons shook his head with a faint smile.

"I absolved Mr. Granger from all suspicion immediately, Parker. You really must learn to apply your grey cells in the approved manner. There was ample opportunity for Mr. Granger to have used either of the two Mausoleum keys, which were in a locked drawer in his desk. So why would he need to draw attention to himself by staging robberies? Even more ludicrous for him to go to Home Farm to burgle Captain Mannering's desk. Things began to point toward Mr. Thaddeus Grimpton but it was not until the legend of the money was mentioned that the missing motive was supplied. My suspicions crystallised from that point, strengthened by mention of the prison visiting. I decided to test my theory by announcing my withdrawal from the case and its solution by Inspector Morgan, with the tragic result we have seen."

"But why did Grimpton go there so unwittingly after Stokoe's death, Pons?"

"That we shall never know, my dear fellow. But he must have been desperate. It was obvious to him that Stokoe was after the money himself, because of the duplicate key. He might perhaps have felt that Stokoe had recruited one of the gypsies; that the two men had quarrelled and that the man with him had knifed him and fled. This was extremely plausible, as we all know. And was obviously reinforced with the arrest of Smith. But he knew that he had to act fast and resolved to try to remove the money himself. That was what I relied upon when I staged our little charade which ended in such a macabre manner. It was his first opportunity to re-visit the Mausoleum since the police had been called in."

"It does not dispose of the central enigma, Pons."

"And what might that be, my dear Parker?"

"Old Brimstone Grimpton's motive in all this, Pons. He amassed a second fortune, which he secreted. He guarded it with that abominable instrument which Mr. Grimpton has just had dismantled. But he apparently made no mention of this treasure in his will."

Solar Pons smiled a strange smile.

"I have the benefit of hindsight there, Parker. I have been browsing through the old man's papers and diaries, with our host's permission, since the conclusion of the case. I have found some curious things. Money was a religion with him. He not only worshipped it but felt somehow that wealth could transcend even the snuffing out of life upon this earth."

"You cannot mean it, Pons!"

"But I do mean it, Parker. His beliefs were basically those of the Ancient Egyptians, and paralleled exactly by his underground treasure house, which mirrored that race's burial customs. The money was for his own use and that of his wife in the after-life."

There was a long silence in the room, broken at last by Septimus Grimpton.

"I think you ought to know, Mr. Pons, that part of the money will be used for various charities, including those for the welfare of ex-prisoners and gypsies."

"Remarkably appropriate, Mr. Grimpton," said Solar Pons, rising from the table. "But I think we should be on our way back to Bath. If I could trouble you for a lift, Inspector?"

"Certainly, Mr. Pons. It has been an education."

Grimpton rose too and pumped Pons' hand warmly.

"I will be in to see you in a day or two, Mr. Pons."

"It will be a pleasure, Mr. Grimpton. And now we really must sample more of the delights of Bath. I think we should stay on for a further week in view of the brighter weather. After all, it has not been much of a holiday for you so far, Parker. And you have not yet taken the waters."

THE ADVENTURE OF
THE BAFFLED BARON

✍ 1

"AH, PARKER, I see that our old friend Jamison is in difficulties again."

"You have the advantage of me, Pons."

"Naturally. You do not command a very good view of the window from your position at the breakfast table. And the casements opposite are making an excellent reflector for the sunshine, which penetrates even into the interior of the police car."

It was a beautiful morning in early June and my friend Solar Pons was standing smoking a reflective after-breakfast pipe at the window of our sitting room at 7B Praed Street.

I remained sitting at the table and spread some more marmalade on my second slice of toast.

"He is exploiting your talents, Pons."

"Possibly, Parker, possibly. Though it would not do to underestimate the doggedness of Inspector Jamison. Obtuse he may be occasionally; and plodding certainly; but method and devotion of duty usually get him to his destination in the end."

"You are being unusually generous this morning, Pons."

"Am I not, Parker?"

Solar Pons smiled amiably.

"But then it is such a superb morning and London has been extremely dull of late. Jamison's arrival may mean action and opportunity. I have been chafing at the bit this last week and our somewhat heavy-footed colleague may unlock the gates for us. You have no objection, I take it?"

"I, Pons? Most certainly not. I am taking a sabbatical today in any case."

"Excellent, Parker. You are usually on your rounds by this time. Ah, here is Mrs. Johnson at the door now."

The beaming, well-scrubbed face of our excellent landlady had indeed appeared round the panel and at Pons' crisp summons to enter she ushered in the worried-looking figure of Inspector Jamison. Pons had already thrown off his old grey dressing-gown and donned his jacket and now he strode forward, his face alert and quite transfigured from its languid expression of a few minutes earlier.

"Welcome, Jamison. Will you not have some coffee?"

"Thank you, Mr. Pons. It has been a week and a half I can tell you."

The Scotland Yard man sank into an armchair indicated by Pons and mopped his brow with a polka-dot handkerchief. His sallow face was beaded with perspiration and his complexion looked grey.

"You need a holiday, Inspector," I suggested.

Jamison gave a wry smile as he put his handkerchief back in his pocket.

"You will have your little joke, doctor."

Mrs. Johnson had withdrawn to her own quarters and Pons passed the big cup of black coffee over to Jamison who seized it as though he had not taken nourishment for a fortnight.

"Trouble?"

Inspector Jamison nodded, a gloomy expression on his face. "Difficulties, Mr. Pons. I should be glad of a little help."

"This agency exists to assist the forces of law and order, Jamison. Pray be more specific."

Solar Pons drew up a chair to the table opposite the Inspector and tented his fingers before him, while his deep-set eyes searched our visitor's face.

"It is a crime of capital dimensions; it has happened within the past twenty-four hours; and there is great pressure on you from above."

Jamison's face turned a mottled colour.

"How did you know that, Mr. Pons?" he snapped.

Solar Pons smiled.

"It is obvious, Jamison. You would not seek my advice unless it were important. Similarly, the same set of criteria apply if you are stuck in your investigations. I estimate it would take you no more than twenty-four hours to conclude that the matter is beyond you. So with pressure on you from above—perhaps from Superintendent Heathfield or even the Commissioner himself—you come to me."

There were dull red patches burning on Jamison's cheeks now.

"You have an unfortunate way of putting it, Mr. Pons," he mumbled. "But basically you are correct."

Solar Pons leaned back in his chair, a thin smile on his face.

"What is the problem?"

Jamison put down his coffee cup on the table with a thin clink in the silence.

"Romane Schneider is dead, Mr. Pons."

Pons looked at Jamison in silence, his brows drawn, while my own astonishment must have shown on my face.

"The sculptor, Inspector? The one who has the International Exhibition on in London at the present time?"

"One and the same, Dr. Parker. Though I know little of such matters he is described as the greatest sculptor this country has ever produced."

Solar Pons' eyes were sparkling and he looked at our visitor piercingly from beneath the lids.

"How did he die, Jamison?"

"Murdered, Mr. Pons. In his own studio in Hampstead. Done to death with one of the mallets he used for his sculpture work."

There was something so evocative in Jamison's hushed tones as he came to the last sentence that an involuntary shudder passed through me.

"When was this?" asked Solar Pons, opening his eyes.

"The early hours of this morning, Mr. Pons. It will be in all tomorrow's editions.

He paused and looked uncomfortable.

"It was a sore point with me, Mr. Pons. I will be quite frank. It took me only a few hours to see that the matter presented certain difficulties."

"Which has brought you here at breakfast-time?"

"Exactly."

Jamison took out his handkerchief again and mopped the nape of his neck with it.

"I have seldom seen a more pointless sort of crime, Mr. Pons. There was no robbery as far as we can make out; no one had a motive; and the studio had not been broken into."

Solar Pons shook his head, a reproving expression on his face.

"Come, Jamison. How many times have I told you? No visible motive. There is always a motive for every crime, however pointless it may appear to the casual bystander."

"You are undoubtedly right, Mr. Pons. But I have seldom been faced with such difficulties. Could you spare the time to step around?"

"Certainly. But first I should like to know a little more about the details. We have time for that, I should imagine?"

"Certainly, Mr. Pons," said Jamison gloomily. "Whoever murdered Romane Schneider will be miles away by now."

Pons held up his finger reprovingly.

"We do not know that, Inspector. And it is useless to speculate without sufficient data."

He looked across at me with satisfaction.

"And as the crime was committed only a few hours ago it means that the trail is fresh."

"You may well be right, Mr. Pons," Jamison went on lugubriously.

"Come, Jamison," said Pons cheerfully. "I have never seen you so down. Pray favour us with some facts."

Jamison put his handkerchief away for the second time and frowned at me before turning his attention to my companion.

"A patrolling constable found the body of Mr. Schneider at three o'clock this morning, Mr. Pons. He saw the light from the skylight. Mr. Schneider lives in a big house in the Vale of Health, which is just off Hampstead High Street."

"Yes, yes, Jamison," said Pons irritably. "I am tolerably familiar with the area. Get to the facts and leave the guide-book details to friend Parker here when he comes to write up the case."

He smiled wryly, ignoring Jamison's frown of discomfiture.

"Very well, Mr. Pons," he continued in a weary voice. "P.C. Daniels would not normally have bothered about a solitary light at that time of the morning except that he knows the area;

knows the house; and also knows that Mr. Schneider rarely works by artificial light; and never after ten o'clock in the evening. He is a man of very fixed personal habits. Or was."

"I see."

Solar Pons' eyes were very steady and piercing as he stared at the Inspector.

"So he decided to investigate the light, Mr. Pons. He did not want to arouse the house, which was in darkness. It is a Georgian building and he walked to the back, through the extensive garden to where the studio stands. It is a detached building of some size. It has a garage and store-rooms at the bottom and a timber staircase and balcony which give access to the studio on the first floor."

"I think I know the house, Pons," I put in. "Cheneys, is it not?"

Inspector Jamison nodded.

"Correct, Dr. Parker. You have an excellent memory."

"It is improving, Jamison," said Pons. "I give you that. You were saying?"

"P.C. Daniels walked up the stairs, Mr. Pons, and knocked. He received no reply. The door was locked so he went round the verandah. There were thick curtains over the windows on the far side. What he saw through a chink in the coverings brought him back to the front where he broke the glass-panelled door in to gain admission. What he found inside made him so sick that he had to come out again for air."

"Heavens!" I exclaimed. "Shocking, was it?"

Jamison nodded.

"Horrible, doctor. Mr. Schneider had been badly battered about the head with one of his own mallets as though by a maniac. So ferocious was the attack that there was blood all over the room; on the base of a statue on which he had been working; and the handle of the mallet itself, though of thick wood, had been clean snapped off. There were no finger-prints, as the murderer had worn gloves."

Solar Pons leaned forward in his chair, thin plumes of smoke from his pipe ascending to the sitting-room ceiling in the still June air.

"You intrigue me, Jamison. I take it the body is still in situ?"

Jamison nodded.

"Nothing has been disturbed, Mr. Pons. Our own people have been there, of course, but we have used extreme care."

Solar Pons rubbed his thin hands together

"Excellent, Jamison. To what conclusion did your constable come?"

"He very wisely telephoned his own station, Mr. Pons, and the C.I.D. were soon out there under a very experienced man named Mooney. He got on to the Yard within the hour, not only because Schneider was such a famous man but because of the extraordinary circumstances."

"Pray tell me about them."

Jamison shrugged.

"I hardly know where to begin, Mr. Pons. We did not arouse the household at that time of the morning and carried out our preliminary investigations as quietly as possible. Our police doctor confirmed that Schneider died earlier that evening, of shock and haemorrhage when the skull was crushed with the first blow. The door of the studio was locked and there was no key; we found no signs on the staircase or door that would indicate forcible entry. The skylight is more than twenty feet from the floor and was locked. Moreover, there are no other entrances and exits and the only key to the door known to be in existence was in the dead man's waistcoat pocket."

"You intrigue me, Jamison."

"I am glad you are able to feel so light-hearted about it, Mr. Pons. This, on top of all my other current cases, beats everything."

"If you did not rouse the household, how did you know that Schneider had the only key?"

Inspector Jamison looked smug.

"For the very good reason, Mr. Pons, that we kept details of the house in a book at the local police station. It is standard routine where there is much valuable property on a particular premises. Mr. Schneider asked our local people to keep an eye on the house and studio, and he always notifies them when he goes on holiday. They asked for a spare key but though he supplied them with one for the house he refused in the case of the studio, emphasising that he had the only one, which was never off his person."

"I see. What about the floor of the studio, Jamison?"

"We thought about that. Heavy tongued and grooved pine throughout, highly polished; with a platform for sitters up at one end."

"Hmm."

Solar Pons rubbed his chin thoughtfully.

"And the garage and store-rooms underneath?"

"Nothing, Mr. Pons. I looked through the garage window with a torch soon after I arrived on the scene but it has a solid cement ceiling. So far as I can make out, the storehouses are crammed from floor to ceiling with crates and packing cases."

"So you have not yet appraised the household of Mr. Schneider's death?"

"That is correct, Mr. Pons. But my colleague, Inspector Buckfast, intended to do so. At a reasonable hour, of course, when the occupants were up and about. Mr. Schneider was a bachelor and had only a secretary and housekeeper living on the premises."

Jamison glanced at his watch.

"He would have done so by now at any rate. And we may well learn more from them. Schneider had enemies, I should imagine."

Pons' face bore the alert and keen look that I had observed so often.

"Ah! Whom, for example?"

The Inspector shook his head.

"Every man in the artistic world and especially a pre-eminent man like Mr. Schneider had them, Mr. Pons. Ranging from the critics to fellow artists."

Jamison had a self-satisfied expression on his features as he sat facing Pons and I could see my companion had a small crease of humour at each corner of his mouth.

"I am much obliged to you for the lecture, Inspector. I had no idea that you were so well-informed in such matters. But you no doubt discovered something in his studio to give you that impression?"

Inspector Jamison looked uncomfortable.

"Well, that is so, Mr. Pons. I took the opportunity of perusing the brochure of Mr. Schneider's current Exhibition while I was there. It had fully documented notes on his career."

Solar Pons smiled.

"You have been most frank, Jamison. It does you credit."

He looked across at me.

"Well, Parker, as it is your day off and you have nothing better to do, perhaps you would care to step around with me? It is not often that Inspector Jamison is at such a dead end and I am feeling unusually public-spirited on such a beautiful morning."

2

A short drive through relatively traffic-free streets brought us to the scene of the tragedy. We turned off Hampstead High Street and drove uphill for a short distance through the Vale of Health. The entrance to Cheneys was in a small lane and the house itself, trim and sparkling with white paint and yellow front door, looked prosperous and cheerful across the soft arc of the green.

Jamison ordered the driver to stop a little distance away and we walked in the welcome shade of leafy trees up to a driveway which led down the side of the house. There was another police car parked nearby and a thin, sandy-haired man in a dark brown suit, with a worried expression on his face, came hurrying down toward us as soon as we were seen.

"This business gets stranger every minute, Inspector," he said curtly.

His faded blue eyes looked curiously at us.

"This is Mr. Solar Pons and his colleague, Dr. Lyndon Parker," said Jamison by way of introduction. "My associate, Inspector Buckfast."

"Delighted to meet you both, gentlemen."

Buckfast's expression was cordial and friendly but the worried look remained. He fell into step with us as we walked along the side of the house, ignoring the salute of the constable stationed in the driveway.

"Something wrong?" queried Jamison.

The other man scratched his head.

"I went to the house about an hour ago. Apparently Schneider rented it to some people called Gantley six months ago. They have no connection with him. They have the use of the building below the studio but Schneider naturally retained the latter for himself. From what I gather Schneider suffered some financial reverses and decided to let. He himself now rents a smaller house on the other side of the Heath."

Jamison raised his eyebrows.

"That puts a different complexion on the matter. Have the Gantleys anything to tell us?"

Buckfast shook his head.

"They see Schneider come and go from time to time, of course. They were most helpful but they neither saw nor heard anything last night. I have not told them of the tragedy, of course. They think there has been a burglary."

Inspector Jamison nodded his head in satisfaction.

"I should like a look at the rest of the studio block, nevertheless."

"There is no difficulty about that. I have the keys."

Jamison turned to us.

"Which would you like to see first, Mr. Pons?"

"Oh, the studio, of course. The garage can come later, though I fancy it will tell us little if you have already examined it."

The studio block itself was a handsome, timbered structure, built of stone in rustic style for the lower portion and with mock Tudor beams in the upper. Jamison led the way up the wide teak staircase, pointing out the massive doors to the garage and store-rooms as we ascended. After a short distance the staircase turned at right-angles, terminating in a covered landing with glass windows.

A constable was on guard at the carved oak door and we went through into a large lobby which contained some coats and hats, together with dusty smocks hanging on pegs; a heavy door-mat; and some canes and walking sticks in a rack. There was a large, gilt-framed mirror, full-length, hanging on the far wall.

Jamison pushed open the inner door and we were soon able fully to realise the horror of the situation which had confronted P.C. Daniels in the small hours of the night.

The studio was a high, long room with white walls and oak beams set diagonally. It was lit from a vast circular skylight about twenty-five feet overhead and there were several hanging lamps of antique pattern but wired for electricity, suspended from the ceiling. The floor was made of heavy pine planking, as Jamison had said, and was evidently buttressed from the store-rooms below to take the enormous weight of the masses of sculpture set about on metal plates and in various stages of completion.

There was a large platform up at one end of the room, approached by shallow steps, and with a polished hand-rail round it. There was an easel on the platform and a drawing board with a hanging lamp above it. There was also a camera on a tripod but my eyes passed over all this at a glance.

Everyone who entered had riveted their gaze on the thing that was sprawled before a piece of white marble sculpture in front of the platform and just a few feet away. The beauty of the statue was in such marked contrast to the awful, bloodied creature lying in an agonised posture beneath it that I think we were all momentarily struck dumb. Even Pons' iron nerve was visibly shaken.

"Venus Aphrodite," he murmured. "This would have been an exquisite piece of work had its creator lived."

Inspector Jamison cleared his throat.

"I don't know about that, Mr. Pons," he murmured. "But she is certainly a beautiful lady."

I caught the faint glimpse of a smile in the mocking glance Pons turned on me at the Inspector's *gaucherie*; that and the marvellous expression on the face of the naked goddess rising from the astonishingly sculptured spray had lightened the moment and I stepped forward briskly as Pons said, "Your department, Parker, I think."

I was already on my knees by the remains of Romane Schneider. He lay with his knees drawn up, his arms outstretched. The fury of the attack had been so great that the whole of the front of the skull had been caved in; death must have been instantaneous. Blood was thickly encrusted in the hair and face and was running from the ears, eyes, mouth and nose.

Great gouts of blood were splashed for yards about the floor and up the base of the statue and the heavy mallet with the broken handle which lay upon the planking was smeared with blood and brains.

I had difficulty in finding a suitable spot in which to kneel with safety but rapidly concluded my examination.

"I agree entirely with the police surgeon's conclusion, Pons," I said. "I can find nothing further."

I rose and dusted my trousers. Pons had already produced the powerful pocket lens, which he habitually carried, and was making a minute examination of the statue, the floor and the immediate area of the body. Jamison and Buckfast stood, a thoughtful group, at the edge of the platform and watched in silence.

Pons straightened up with a grunt.

"The murderer was a man over six feet tall; of enormous strength; but at the same time able to walk as quietly as a cat. The death of Schneider was obviously a matter of great urgency and carried out with technical precision. The motive, when it can be discovered, was so important that it was necessary to eliminate Schneider as rapidly as possible."

I glanced at the two detective officers who were standing open-mouthed upon the platform.

"Come, Pons," I protested. "That the murderer was a man of enormous strength, is fairly obvious. But how do you arrive at your other conclusions?"

"It is surely elementary, Parker," said Solar Pons quietly. "From a careful examination of the body I estimate that Schneider was a man of some five feet eleven inches, perhaps six feet. The single shattering blow that snuffed his life struck him squarely on the crown of the head, carried on into the brain pan and caved in the front of the skull at the same time. To do that the man of normal height, were he tremendously strong, would have to stand upon a box or some form of support. No, Parker, the man who took Schneider's life would need to be at least six feet four inches in height to inflict such a blow. What say you, Jamison?"

The Inspector scratched his head.

"You are certainly correct, Mr. Pons, now that you have pointed it out. We have established Mr. Schneider's height as being five feet eleven."

Solar Pons gave me a thin smile as he turned back to look at the statue of Aphrodite.

"Very well, Pons. But the cat-like qualities?"

"The murderer came from the direction of the door, Parker. To do that he would have to walk a long way. It was obvious that Schneider was at work upon the statue, with his back to the door. Therefore, it was not until his attacker reached him that he became aware of his presence. Will you stand over here, Parker? There, that is correct. Your shadow, as you will notice, is now thrown across the base of the statue. Schneider whirled to receive the mallet blow upon the crown and front of the head. He died instantly."

"That is undoubtedly right, Mr. Pons," said Inspector Buckfast quietly. "But how did his attacker escape?"

"We have yet to establish that, Inspector. But it is obvious that he walked back toward the door. And equally obvious that he dried his shoes at a point here. There was a light rain last night."

Pons walked rapidly to a spot below the railed platform where the two police officers stood and examined the planking minutely with his lens.

"Here, you see, he has wiped his shoes upon the planks. When they were sufficiently dry to leave no marks, he then left. Let us just see..."

Pons moved from board to board, his movements intent and bird-like, his ascetic face alight with concentration. Impressed despite themselves, Jamison and Buckfast remained silent.

"There is a little dust but not enough," said Pons presently, rising from his bent posture. "The traces become illegible halfway between the door and the platform."

He glanced upward at the skylight far above our heads.

"It is possible that he was lowered by a rope from above, though unlikely. We shall want that skylight carefully examined, Jamison."

"We have already done so, Mr. Pons."

"I am aware of that. But the operative word is carefully. I suggest it was done cursorily in the early hours of this morning. Incidentally, why was not P.C. Daniels aware that Schneider had let his house and moved?"

"I have already asked him that, Mr. Pons. He is on nights and would not have been aware of any such move. He usually saw Schneider at the studio or thereabouts. Daniels was sometimes in the habit of trying the studio door in the small hours on his beat."

"Hmm."

Pons stood frowning, tugging at the lobe of his right ear as was his habit in moments of great concentration.

"You have not yet told us why the act was so important, Pons, and how you arrived at the conclusion that Schneider had to be eliminated as soon as possible."

Solar Pons turned his piercing glance upon me.

"Tut, Parker, it is self-evident. Learn to use your own ratiocinative faculties. The blow proves that. One colossal, shattering stroke that extinguished life in a second. Schneider had to be killed as quickly as possible. That stands out clearly. The murderer obviously seized the nearest tool to hand; the mallet undoubtedly came from this table here, halfway between the door and the statue."

"You are right, Pons, as always," I muttered.

Solar Pons smiled thinly.

"Right on this occasion, Parker. I am not always so, as I would be the first to admit."

"But could it not have been jealousy or some mad rage, Pons?"

My friend shook his head.

"A jealous rival you mean? A feud in the artistic world? It is barely possible. A person in a mad rage would have gone on battering at the body long after life was extinct. But this was one devastating blow. One would say a clean blow if it had not left such an abattoir-like aftermath."

He looked round with distaste, turning his gaze up to the two silent men in front of us.

"You are right in one thing, Jamison. This is a case which presents a number of baffling aspects. We will just look at the storerooms below before questioning the occupants of the house."

3

"There is little to see here, Pons."

"I am inclined to agree with you, my dear Parker. But even a negative result tends to eliminate the possibility of error."

We stood in the garage below the studio, Inspector Jamison gloomily behind us. Inspector Buckfast had excused himself and gone back to Cheneys to warn the occupants of our impending arrival.

As Jamison had already told us, the roof of the garage was made of metal girders and cement and there was obviously no way into the studio from the ground. As I moved aimlessly about the floor, noting the Rolls-Royce Silver Ghost and the other opulent touring car in the interior, my mind was overcome by the obvious difficulties in reconciling the facts of Romane Schneider's death. There was no way into the studio; there was no reason to believe there had ever been a second key to the front door; and Pons had already ascertained that the door in question had not been tampered with.

Even as the thought crossed my mind there was a shadow at the garage entrance and a plain-clothes man reported to Inspector Jamison, "The skylight has obviously not been opened for several years, sir. It is secured with heavy bolts from the inside and when we tried to open it, we found the framing screwed down."

Inspector Jamison thanked his subordinate and turned to Pons, his lugubrious features even more grave.

"It just gets more difficult, Mr. Pons."

"On the contrary, light is beginning to show, Jamison. By blocking it out we must eventually arrive at one compact beam which will illuminate the truth for us."

Jamison frowned at me.

"Very picturesquely put, Mr. Pons. Let us just hope you are right."

He led the way through a connecting door in the wall of the garage to a large storage area on the right. This was divided into brick bays and the place was, as Jamison had already told us, jammed from floor to ceiling with crates and boxes. Pons looked keenly about him in the shadowy light. It was difficult to see the thick pine boarding but it was evident that the ceiling was solid and heavy. Moreover, the crates in the bays extended to within an inch or so of the woodwork overhead.

"Just as I told you, Mr. Pons," said the Inspector.

"What is in these boxes, Inspector?"

"I understand from Buckfast that Colonel Gantley, the gentleman who has leased Cheneys, is an antique dealer and importer of curios. Some of the stuff is very valuable, according to Buckfast; while other material is oriental workmanship of no very great value imported into the country for the Colonel's business. He has a shop in Hampstead High Street, which was why he wanted to move nearer his premises."

"Just so," said Pons languidly, looking through half-closed eyes at the legends stencilled on the wooden boxes immediately in front of us.

"The gentleman certainly seems to have very extensive sources, Parker. Hong Kong, Manila, Singapore, Peking and Hangkow are just a few of the names I see before me."

He stepped round a bundle of straw and looked sharply at a

small porcelain Buddha which had been unpacked on a rough wooden bench.

"Rather charming work, wouldn't you say so, Parker?"

"Excellent, Pons," I agreed.

Indeed, the workmanship was first-rate and I was surprised to see that the label bore a price of only seven guineas.

"It is astonishingly cheap, Pons."

"Is it not, Parker. But then labour is plentiful in the East, as you are no doubt aware."

"I should not mind that on the mantel at 7B, Pons."

"As you say, Parker, a nice piece. No doubt you may make the Colonel an offer for it when we see him in a moment."

Pons moved away and as he did so his shoes made a harsh, gritty noise on the cement floor of the store-room. Jamison had already turned back to the open air as the thin form of a man came hurrying down the garden toward us, visible through the half-open door. To my astonishment Pons was on his knees, scraping with his fingernails at some white substance on the cement.

My amazement was increased when I saw him tentatively taste it with the extreme tip of his tongue. He put his hand back in his pocket, turned to me and then we were walking up the garden to meet the hurrying figure, before I had time to make any comment on this strange behaviour.

Colonel Gantley turned out to be a tall, fussy-looking man in his early sixties with whitening hair and a frayed silver moustache. He had deep furrows at the corners of his mouth that made his yellow face look like something out of one of those plays set on tropical islands which were becoming the vogue in the West End. He wore a lightweight drill suit with military-style buttons and his brown eyes twinkled benevolently from behind silver-rimmed spectacles.

"A disturbing business, gentlemen," he said briskly, as Jamison introduced us. "I hope that nothing has been stolen from my premises."

"They were all secure, sir," said the Inspector. "And thank you for letting us look around."

"Always anxious to assist the police," said the Colonel, clasping my companion by the hand. "Mr. Solar Pons. It is a pleasure, my dear sir. But you are surely not interested in this trifling affair of my neighbour's burglary?"

Pons gave a dry laugh.

"Not at all, Colonel. I am assisting the police in another matter and, needing to consult Inspector Jamison, was told I could find him here."

"I see. Well, I am at your disposal, gentlemen, but I do not think I shall be of much help."

"One never knows," said Jamison mildly. "You heard nothing at all during the night, I understand?"

"Nothing, Inspector. But then I am a very heavy sleeper and my room is at the side of the house. Of course, anyone could have approached the studio by way of the drive. The gates are never locked. Mr. Schneider sometimes leaves at a late hour. I hear his car during the night on occasion."

"Indeed," said Pons casually.

We were strolling back down the garden now in the bright sunlight, the faint hum of the traffic coming from the main road which passed through the Vale of Health.

"You have not contacted Mr. Schneider, then?" said Colonel Gantley.

Inspector Jamison shook his head.

"We have rung his house, of course. But I understand from his secretary that Mr. Schneider is away at present."

"I see. Well, I hope you catch your man. Now, if there is nothing further, I must get back to my business."

"By all means, Colonel. I am sorry to have taken your time."

We shook hands with the Colonel and watched as he strode back down the driveway to where his car was parked in the side road. A few moments later its engine faded into the general traffic noise.

"So much for that, Pons," I observed.

Solar Pons had been silent, idly drawing patterns in the dust at his feet with the toe of his shoe.

"As you say, Parker."

Jamison frowned, screwing up his eyes against the strong light.

"What next, Mr. Pons?"

"I really think a call at Mr. Schneider's private residence is indicated, Jamison."

"Just as you say, Mr. Pons."

Schneider's new address proved to be a narrow-chested three-storey house of mellow red brick, just off the bustle of Hampstead High Street. The brass fittings of the red front door sparkled in the sunlight and in the small front garden I recognised a granite phoenix created by Schneider, which had once been exhibited at the Paris Exposition.

The door was opened for us by Inspector Buckfast, who had preceded his colleague. He jerked his thumb back over his shoulder.

"I have just told his secretary, Godfrey Horrabin. He has taken it badly. The housekeeper, Mrs. Biggins, is resting in her room."

Jamison nodded without speaking and a moment later Buckfast led the way down a thickly carpeted corridor to a well-appointed study where the secretary was waiting.

Godfrey Horrabin turned out to be a dark-haired man of about thirty, with an ashen-white face and full lips from which the colour had now fled. He rose from his employer's desk as we entered and I then realised he was of an enormous height, well over six feet tall. I shot a significant glance at Pons but he appeared to be occupied in looking about him at the contents of the study as Buckfast introduced us.

"I am sorry, gentlemen, but this has been a dreadful shock. A dreadful shock."

Horrabin slumped back into his chair and passed a handkerchief over his face. Pons sat down opposite him at the other side of the desk and looked at him sympathetically.

"I quite understand, Mr. Horrabin. These things tend to fell one at the time. You'll forgive me, Jamison, for asking the questions."

"Go ahead, Mr. Pons."

Jamison and I sat down in padded leather chairs which were set near the desk and I looked round curiously as Horrabin fought to control his feelings.

"You have been with Mr. Schneider how long?"

"For the past five years, Mr. Pons."

"So that you know him and his habits fairly well?"

"As well as anyone could, I should imagine."

The secretary replaced the handkerchief in the breast pocket of his blue jacket and appeared more composed.

"Was he a tempestuous man? One who would have made many enemies in the course of his career?"

The secretary gave a faint smile which momentarily lightened his features.

"Like most artists he was extremely temperamental. He had been involved in some tremendous arguments and on occasion in actual physical violence."

Pons' eyes were fixed on the secretary's face. He tented his fingers before him and leaned back in his chair, his whole figure expressing dynamic energy.

"Tell me about it, Mr. Horrabin."

The secretary shrugged.

"It is a well-known story, Mr. Pons. A famous rivalry between two sculptors. I have known them take each other's mallets and actually demolish portions of each other's work with which they were offended."

"Indeed."

Solar Pons' eyes were sparkling now.

"You are referring to Sir Hercules Kronfeld, I take it?"

Horrabin looked surprised.

"You knew about it, Mr. Pons?"

My friend chuckled.

"One could hardly avoid it. I would not say that the world of sculpture is one with which I am entirely *au fait*. But I do read the newspapers assiduously and I do seem to remember an item about two years ago when the couple were engaged in a *fracas* at the Paris Salon."

"You are perfectly right, Mr. Pons. They were once good friends but their rivalry developed to such an extent that one could say that only hatred kept them together."

"An extremely apt summing-up," said Solar Pons. "And one that might well apply to many marriages. Eh, Parker?"

"No doubt you are right, Pons."

Solar Pons cupped his lean fingers round his right knee and rocked to and fro as he regarded the secretary keenly.

"You have opened up a fruitful field for investigation, Mr. Horrabin. Are there any other people to whom you would particularly wish to draw my attention?"

The secretary shook his head.

"I cannot think of any, Mr. Pons. There were a number of rows, of course. Various critics and journalists displeased Mr. Schneider from time to time. But the feud with Sir Hercules is the one which stands out."

Pons nodded, tugging at the lobe of his right ear.

"Is Sir Hercules in London, do you know?"

"I believe so, Mr. Pons. He actually telephoned Mr. Schneider a few days ago. He lives in Chelsea. I will get you the address."

"Thank you, Mr. Horrabin. And now, if you will excuse us, I would just like to look around this study for half an hour or so."

"Certainly, Mr. Pons. You have only to press that button there if you require my services. It is connected directly with my quarters."

He pointed to a brass bell-push set into the surface of the desk and quitted the room. Solar Pons sat quietly for a moment, before searching in his pocket for his pipe. He turned to the Inspector as he lit it.

"What do you make of that, Jamison?"

The Inspector wrinkled his brow. The three of us were alone in the room now, Inspector Buckfast having left us at the door. I could see him through the window, painstakingly quartering the garden outside, scrutinising every inch of pathway and turf.

"You mean his size, Mr. Pons?"

Jamison's face lightened for the first time since he had requested Pons' help.

"Well, he is certainly big enough, Mr. Pons. He fits the bill."

"I did not say he did it, Inspector. But it is a possibility which we must not overlook. It is motive which interests me at the moment. And after all, London is full of men who are more than six feet tall. It is the ones who have been in contact with Mr. Schneider who interest us. What say you, Parker?"

"Just what I was thinking, Pons."

Solar Pons smiled faintly.

"You are ever the receptive listener, Parker. That is an invaluable quality and one consistently underrated by the world."

"You are too good today, Pons."

"It is the weather, Parker. I find the combination of such a day and a case of this complexity irresistible."

Inspector Jamison threw up his hands and looked at me helplessly but Pons was already on his feet, his smile intensified, as he went rapidly back and forth across the shelves of the dead man's study.

We waited silently as he continued with his examination. He paused in front of a row of letter files and lifted one out. He put it down with a grunt and started to go through the contents. Soon he had three open on the desk before him. He threw a bundle of envelopes over to me.

"What do you make of those, Parker?"

I scanned the contents with rising agitation, passing them to Jamison before I had finished.

"Why, these are love-letters, Pons!" I said with indignation. "And not to put too fine a point on it, the man sounds an unmitigated swine!"

"Does he not, Parker," said Solar Pons with a dry chuckle. "Letters from a wide variety of different women, most of them with a grudge. And significantly, the studio has been used as a rendezvous, it seems clear."

"A deplorable business, Pons."

Solar Pons pulled at the lobe of his left ear and regarded me thoughtfully.

"You take an altogether too moralistic view of the world, Parker, if you do not mind me saying so. An artist of Mr. Schneider's calibre and one barely into his fifties would be bound to attract the attention of women. A famous name is like a magnet to a certain type of feminine personality."

"For a bachelor you seem to know quite a bit about it, Mr. Pons," put in Jamison sourly.

Creases of amusement appeared at the corners of Solar Pons' mouth.

"A touch, a distinct touch, Jamison," he murmured. "But as Dr. Johnson once said, a man does not have to be a carpenter to criticise a table. These letters raise a number of interesting possibilities."

I stared at Pons as he went on sifting through the correspondence in the files on the desk before him.

"Surely, Pons," I began. "You do not mean to say a woman committed this crime?"

Solar Pons shook his head.

"I hardly think so, Parker. It is not a woman's type of crime. The female mind is far more subtle, which is why we have so many lady poisoners in the annals of murder. And I hardly think a woman would have had the strength to strike Schneider in that fashion. She would have had to have been an Amazon indeed. And as I have already indicated, there would have been a multiplicity of blows in the case of a jealous rage. Even Inspector Jamison here referred to a battering when he consulted me. Yet we have one blow only."

"That was an error on my part, Mr. Pons," Jamison put in. "It is still difficult for me to believe such damage could be inflicted on the human frame with a single stroke."

Solar Pons put the files back on the shelves and sat down at the desk.

"Nevertheless, these letters are of considerable interest."

Light broke in.

"You mean a jealous husband might have killed his wife's lover, Pons!"

"It is not outside the bounds of possibility, Parker. I have not yet made up my mind. But now, if you are ready, Inspector, we shall see what Sir Hercules Kronfeld has to say for himself."

4

Our destination was one of those tall, elegant and extremely expensive houses in Cheyne Walk, which command a magnificent view of the Thames frontage and Chelsea Bridge from the topmost windows. Our driver pulled in from the traffic stream and we walked up the leafy crescent to a large house in the middle which, to gather from the white trellis-work sparkling in the sunshine, boasted an extensive roof-garden.

"Sir Hercules appears to live in some style, Pons," I observed.

"Does he not, Parker. It would seem that his star is in the ascendant whereas, if Colonel Gantley's information be correct, Mr. Schneider's was waning. If not from an artistic, certainly from a financial point of view."

"It is often the case, Pons, in the world of the arts."

"You astonish me with your knowledge of such matters, Parker," said Solar Pons gravely.

His ring at the front door bell brought a trim little maid in her early twenties, an appealing sight with her lace collar and cuffs and bobbed dark hair; and we were speedily shown through an elegant suite of rooms to Sir Hercules' studio. This was a spacious room on the second floor with a huge skylight and large oval window to admit the north light.

Sir Hercules himself was a gigantic figure with a beard heavily flecked with grey. Contrary to my expectations he was elegantly dressed in a light grey suit and blue bow-tie and his fresh complexion and careful grooming completely belied the conventional picture of the artist. He was leaning carelessly against a winged female nude, evidently one of his own works, while he carried on a murmured conversation with an elegant young man with patent leather hair and a soulful expression.

As we were announced he excused himself to his companion and came striding down the room toward us. So massive was he that the studio seemed to tremble as he advanced. Solar Pons' eyes had a mild twinkle as he gazed at the Inspector. Sir Hercules Kronfeld was close to us now, looking from one to the other with an inquiring expression on his face. He gave a wry chuckle.

"My accountant."

He jerked his thumb in the direction of the figure by the statue. "All the same these young fellows nowadays. They seem to think we're in this for art's sake."

He chuckled again and pumped Inspector Jamison's hand.

"Pleased to meet you, Inspector, though I don't know why I should be so honoured."

"I am sorry for the intrusion, Sir Hercules. This is Mr. Solar Pons and Dr. Lyndon Parker."

The deep brown eyes swivelled and studied us closely.

"It is always interesting for a master in one field to meet a *maître* in another, Mr. Pons."

"You are too good, Sir Hercules."

"We will not keep you a moment, sir," Inspector Jamison

broke in without further preamble. "We have come in the matter of Romane Schneider."

Sir Hercules Kronfeld looked at the Inspector in silence for a moment. His manner was distinctly cooler and little flecks of anger were dancing in his eyes.

"I do not care to hear anything of that unmitigated charlatan, Inspector, and I will thank you not to mention that man's name within the walls of my house."

Jamison reddened but pressed on stolidly.

"I'm afraid we're going to have to mention it, Sir Hercules. This is a Scotland Yard matter."

"Oh."

There was intense curiosity on the sculptor's face.

"What has he been up to now? I should be glad to hear you are on the point of arresting him, but that is too much to hope for."

"You did not like him, then, Sir Hercules?"

"I? I detest him."

"You need do so no longer," interrupted Solar Pons quietly. "He has been murdered in the most brutal and horrifying manner."

A remarkable change had come over Sir Hercules. Pons' words seemed visibly to deflate him. He staggered. His face went white and he moved over toward a wooden stand supporting one of his sculptures, bracing himself with a thick, fleshy hand. His lips moved once or twice but he was unable to articulate the words.

"It seems to be a shock to you," went on Solar Pons calmly. "I have often observed that the removal of an object of hatred may be as traumatic as that of a loved one."

Sir Hercules had recovered himself by now. He cleared his throat harshly.

"Forgive me, gentlemen," he murmured. "It was a shock, I must admit. I hardly know what to say."

"You are unable to help us, then, in the matter of Mr. Schneider's death?" muttered Jamison.

Sir Hercules fixed him with a stern glance.

"I? How on earth could I help? I have not even seen him for three months."

"A pity," the Inspector went on. "I had hoped you might have thrown some light on the matter."

"You must disabuse yourself of that, Inspector. Like me, Schneider had many enemies. It is inevitable in the art world, I am afraid. How did he die?"

"Struck on the head with tremendous force with one of his own mallets. His skull was completely shattered and he must have expired instantaneously."

Sir Hercules Kronfeld drew in his breath with a shuddering sigh.

"Horrible, Inspector. Just horrible. I did not think I could feel so drained."

"I am sorry to be the first to bring you the news. Have you anyone in mind who might have done this dreadful thing?"

Sir Hercules, obviously moved, now had his back turned but faced us again. His lips were trembling and his features were still bleached of all colour.

"No one, Inspector. He had no specific enemies that I know of."

He gave a short, cynical laugh.

"Except myself."

"Pray do not punish yourself, Sir Hercules," said Pons quietly.

The sculptor shot him a shrewd glance.

"You are a remarkable man, Mr. Pons. I can see that the true situation has not escaped you."

Pons smiled wryly.

"We have many examples in the arts. Gilbert and Sullivan in more recent times, of course."

Inspector Jamison had watched this exchange with obvious bewilderment.

"I do not see how this helps us, Mr. Pons," he said heavily.

"Of course not, Inspector," said Solar Pons. "We must be going. We can do no good here and I am sure Sir Hercules has much to occupy him."

He rested his hand lightly on the sculptor's shoulder as he passed. Sir Hercules recollected himself with an effort.

"Good day, gentlemen. You will forgive me for not showing you out."

We were silent as we walked back through the house, preceded by the same parlour-maid who had let us in.

"Well, Mr. Pons," said Inspector Jamison as we regained the street. "A giant of a man. One with strength enough and opportunity enough to commit such a crime. I shall have him carefully watched."

Solar Pons raised his eyebrows.

"Take my advice, Jamison, and direct your attention elsewhere," he advised.

Jamison frowned.

"Come, Mr. Pons," he said. "You are not omniscient. We know Sir Hercules and the dead man were bitter enemies. There is reason enough for the committing of such a crime, surely . . . "

"You have still to explain how Sir Hercules got in and out of that studio like a puff of smoke, Jamison. It really will not do."

Jamison's face assumed a stubborn aspect which I knew of old.

"Nevertheless, Mr. Pons, you must allow me to pursue this affair in my own way."

"Certainly, Inspector. That is your prerogative. I think we have done all we can for the moment, Parker. Allow us to bid you good day, Jamison."

5

"What do you make of it, Parker?"

We were seated in our comfortable sitting-room at 7B Praed Street. Pons had been silent for the last hour, after the tea-things had been cleared away, and the upper air of the room was blue with pipe-smoke.

"You already know my feelings, Pons. It is baffling indeed."

"Nevertheless, I should like to have the benefit of your observations in the matter."

I put down my newspaper and regarded my companion sceptically but there was nothing but concerned interest in his face. Beams of evening sunlight, striking through the windows that overlooked Praed Street, made a scarlet mask of his face as he waited for my reply.

"We have no motive, Pons."

"Exactly."

"We have a studio which was locked and to and from which no one apparently came or went."

"The salient points have not escaped you, my dear fellow."

"The murderer, according to your conclusions, must have been over six feet tall."

"Agreed."

"His greatest enemy, Sir Hercules, fits that physical description."

"So do a great many men."

"His secretary, Godfrey Horrabin, for example, Pons?"

Solar Pons gave a dry chuckle and looked at me mockingly.

"You now have two suspects, Parker. I suggest we may find a third—or even a fourth—before this case is over."

He rose, stretched himself and walked casually across toward the window.

"Are you free to accompany me this evening?"

"Certainly, Pons."

Pons came back from the window and sat down again.

"It is a pity it does not get dark until almost after ten o'clock at this time of the year. It would be better to go there after dark. It would not do to let Colonel Gantley see us in his garden at night. He might suspect us of being burglars."

"What on earth are you talking about, Pons?"

"Nothing, Parker. It is just that I have a mind to look at that studio again. I fancy Jamison will not have the body removed until after dark. Discretion is one of the virtues of the British police, after all."

"But how will we get in, Pons?"

"I took an impression of the key when we were at the studio this morning, Parker. I have had it made up this afternoon."

I stared at Pons in astonishment.

"I fail to see . . ."

"You fail to see, my dear fellow, because you do not draw the correct conclusions from the data before you. You remember the letters we found in Schneider's study?"

"It will be a long time before I forget them, Pons."

"Exactly. Yet those letters told you nothing?"

"That the sculptor, was a cad and an unscrupulous cheat where women were concerned."

"Tut, Parker. We are not concerned with moral strictures. Murder has been done."

"I realise that, Pons."

"The studio was a quiet, discreet place. Schneider was not known to use it at night. He sculptured female nudes there. And he would not give the key to his local police-station."

I stared at my companion for a long moment.

"I see your reasoning, Pons, but I cannot quite grasp the conclusion."

Solar Pons made an irritated clicking noise with his tongue.

"I am bluntly suggesting that Schneider, a successful and well-known sculptor, was quite patently a secret womaniser on an heroic scale. What more likely rendezvous for his amorous intrigues than the studio?"

"I follow that, Pons, but where does that lead us?"

Solar Pons' face expressed sorrowful resignation.

"The studio is altogether too open and simple, like the face of an ingenuous man. There has to be something else beneath it. What more likely a secret entrance so that his lady friends could come and go without being suspected? And also that they be kept from seeing one another if one ever came to the front door? Or their husbands. Do I make myself clear?"

I gulped.

"Good heavens, Pons. It is crystal clear, now that you put it like that. The skylight, perhaps . . . "

Solar Pons laughed. It was not an unkind laugh but it cut nevertheless.

"We must look to the ground, not skywards, Parker. Though

it seems unlikely from the solid construction of the studio, there must be a way in from below."

"Ah, the garage?"

Pons shook his head.

"The ceiling was of solid cement. Most likely the store-room."

I smiled.

"You mean that Schneider's style was cramped by his letting Cheneys to Colonel Gantley? Necessity compelled him to do so. Perhaps he hoped to continue his liaisons but the stacking of the crates for the Colonel's business prevented the use of the secret entrance?"

"It may well be," said Pons airily. "There are a number of intriguing possibilities. Linked, I have no doubt, with the ex-tortionately high rent charged by Schneider for his house."

"I do not follow you, Pons."

"It would not be the first time, Parker. Nevertheless, while going through Schneider's papers today I found some interest-ing documents, obviously overlooked by Jamison and his colleagues. The late Romane Schneider was charging the Colonel £100 a week for the use of Cheneys."

I stared at my companion in stupefaction.

"You cannot mean it, Pons?"

"The figures are there, in black and white, Parker. Intriguing, is it not? However, I suggest we set off. A walk in this agreeable weather will not come amiss. It should be dark by the time we arrive."

A few minutes later, having appraised Mrs. Johnson of our departure, we were walking through the streets of London in the pleasant warmth of a perfect summer evening. It was cool in the shadows of the buildings after the intense heat of the day and my spirits rose as we walked up Gloucester Road in the direction of Hampstead. Traffic was light at this time of the evening and there was a good sprinkling of cyclists so that dust, the plague of the London summer, was at a minimum.

Solar Pons strode out at a great pace, discoursing on a wide variety of topics and I listened with interest, interpolating a question or a monosyllabic remark from time to time. So absorbed were we that I hardly noticed the closing in of dusk but the lamps had just been lit when we at last turned into Hampstead High Street and on to the Vale of Health.

To my surprise Pons stepped aside and led me to a public house, where a few chairs and benches were set outside on the green turf. It was a cool and pleasant spot while we waited for the last of the light to die from the sky. There were but a few bars of blood red lingering in the west and the hill was a lime-yellow glow of gaslights before Pons rose from his seat and started off across the turf.

I was at his heels as he circled round, keeping a sharp eye on Cheneys in its quiet cul-de-sac. There were lights in the upper rooms of the house but so far as I could make out, the studio building at the rear was in darkness.

"Is this likely to be dangerous, Pons?" I asked, as we gained the road at the far side of the green and continued our walk onwards.

"Most decidedly, Parker, if my calculations be correct," said Pons.

"The police appear to have withdrawn and conditions are ideal."

"For what, Pons?"

"For our purpose, my dear fellow."

"Perhaps I should have brought my revolver?"

"I had not overlooked it, Parker. Thinking that you might need it I took the liberty of bringing it along."

And Solar Pons produced the weapon from the inside of his jacket pocket with a thin smile.

"Really, Pons!" I protested, thrusting it into my pocket. "I sometimes think you must be clairvoyant."

"Hardly, Parker. Merely thoughtful, but I do sympathise with your feelings."

We had turned again now and I was aware of a gigantic figure silhouetted against the gas-lamps in front of us.

"Good evening, Mr. Pons. Thought I might find you here, sir."

The police constable touched the peak of his helmet and came to a stop in front of us. So huge was he that he towered over Solar Pons, despite his own not inconsiderable height.

"Ah, P.C. Daniels, is it not? The man who found the body?"

"Nasty business, Mr. Pons. I understood from Inspector Jamison that you had been consulted. I have not seen you, sir, since that murderous affair in Paddington. Right on your own doorstep."

"Ah, the anarchists," said Pons, his keen eyes searching the giant's face. "I have not forgotten your services on that occasion. And in any event your remarkable physique makes you a difficult man to forget."

The constable laughed shortly. He was a man of about thirty with a heavy black moustache which stood out like a great bar of shadow on his alert, intelligent face.

"I must admit there are not many things I fear on night beat, Mr. Pons, but that business of Mr. Schneider gave me a nasty turn."

"I can well imagine, constable. Tell me, has the body yet been removed?"

"Not twenty minutes since, Mr. Pons. You have just missed Inspector Jamison. Did you wish to gain entry to the studio, sir? The Inspector has the only key."

"It is no matter, Daniels. I was merely mulling over some problems in my mind. By the bye, I have not yet seen anything of the murder in the early editions this afternoon?"

The constable shook his head.

"It is being handled very discreetly, Mr. Pons. Inspector Jamison has not made any announcement as yet, though I have no doubt the newspapers will have got hold of it by this time tomorrow."

"No doubt. Well, I must not keep you, Daniels. Goodnight to you."

"Goodnight, sir."

The constable touched the brim of his helmet again and moved off in the dusk, like an amiable but potentially dangerous bear. I looked after him thoughtfully, conscious of Pons' eyes on me.

"Formidable is he not, Parker?"

"Yes, Pons. Gracious, you surely do not suspect him of the crime?"

"It has been done before, Parker. Notably in a work by G.K. Chesterton. But I do not think that nature is imitating art in this case. I am merely pointing out that we begin to have a plethora of huge men in this case. Daniels is the third. Perhaps we may have more luck with the fourth."

"I am becoming more and more confused, Pons," I said. "One would have thought the singularity of the crime in the locked studio, let alone the height of the murderer, would have simplified matters. Instead, we have a multiplicity of suspects."

Pons chuckled drily.

"Have we not, Parker. But I think light is about to break."

6

And he said nothing more until we had skirted the bright windows of Cheneys and were standing within the deep shadow of the back garden. We cautiously crossed the lawn and once again came out on the paved concourse fronting the garage and storeroom block below the studio. The moon was shining brightly and reflected a metallic sheen from the great domed skylight of the studio.

"I would give a great deal to have been at that skylight when Schneider was attacked, Pons," I whispered.

Solar Pons nodded.

"Each to his own last, my dear fellow. You would have robbed me of a most fascinating problem had you done so."

He put his hand on my arm and drew me over toward the garage door. To my surprise he produced a metal instrument from his pocket and bent over the padlock. A minute or two passed and then there was a faint click. Pons turned to me.

"Now, inside with you, Parker, and be quiet about it."

I slipped through the door and waited until he had softly closed it behind us, leaving the padlock hanging from the hasp outside.

"I thought we were going into the studio, Pons," I whispered.

"Later, Parker. You forget the crates in here. It would not do to wreck the Colonel's precious imports."

I nodded, following close behind as Pons tip-toed through

the garage, past the bulky forms of the two automobiles it contained. As we had seen that morning, there was a connecting door to the store-room, which was unlocked. Solar Pons led the way to the far wall and gazed up through the gloom at the piled boxes which climbed toward the ceiling.

"This will be a difficult job, Pons."

My companion shook his head.

"I think not, Parker, if my suppositions be correct. Just place that large box at the foot here, will you."

I helped him slide the crate over. Solar Pons fingered the lobe of his left ear and looked at me reflectively in the gloom.

"Just as I thought, my dear fellow. A natural staircase."

I soon saw what he meant, for he simply marched up the slope of heavy boxes, which were arranged in tiers, rather like steps. I followed and joined him on the topmost crate.

"What now, Pons?"

"Nothing could be simpler, Parker."

So saying he pulled at the large boxes in front of him, which stretched from the crates to the ceiling. I gasped, for the enormous pile, at least ten feet high, came away with the utmost ease, Pons holding the lowest between the tips of his fingers. He chuckled at my expression.

"As I suspected. Mere cardboard, Parker, glued together. You will see that there is nothing between the crates on which we are standing and the floor yonder. Just help me with these other piles."

In a few minutes we had removed all four piles of boxes, and placed them lower down. We now had a clear space from floor to ceiling, revealing a large expanse of concrete at the rear of the wooden crates. Pons glanced keenly at the slatted wooden ceiling revealed.

"We can learn nothing further here, Parker. The answer must lie in the studio above. Come."

Gaining the outside and first making sure that there was no one else in the garden, Pons crept quietly up the staircase to the studio. I followed quickly, just in time to see the lean form of my friend glide through the door, which he had swiftly opened with the duplicate key. I moved toward the light switch but Pons instantly stopped me.

"I think not, Parker. It is annoying, I know, and will make the task doubly tedious but we must work without the benefit of the main light."

He moved over cautiously through the studio into which silvery moonlight was filtering from the skylight above. The body of the unfortunate sculptor had been removed, as P.C. Daniels had told us, but the tarpaulin which covered the spot where he had lain and the gouts of blood upon the statue of Venus Aphrodite were a vivid reminder of the brooding horror of that moment when we had first entered the chamber of death.

Pons had a small pocket torch out now and was moving cautiously across the planking of the floor. To my surprise he ignored the main studio and went up the shallow staircase to the platform where the easel stood. Pons remained musing for a moment, his right hand stroking his chin, while the beam from his torch played quickly up and down the flooring.

"Why do you feel any entrance must be here, Pons?" I whispered.

"Simply because there is no other place, Parker," said Solar Pons. "The crates below are solid, except for those we have just removed. The corner of the cleared area corresponds to this platform here. Besides, the buttressed sections below would not allow it."

"I saw no buttresses, Pons."

"Because you were not looking for them, my dear fellow. There were several steel beams, against which boxes and crates had been stacked for the purposes of Colonel Gantley's antique business. We must not forget the enormous weight of these sculptures."

"But I cannot possibly see how there could be an entrance, Pons. As we have just noted the ceiling below here is solid."

Solar Pons turned to me. In the dim light of the torch his eyes were twinkling.

"I have already pointed out, Parker, there must be an entrance. Otherwise, Romane Schneider would still be alive. You really must learn to eliminate all inessentials."

He turned from me and gave an experimental tug on the cord by which the overhead light was suspended. Satisfied, he moved over to the polished wooden railing that surrounded the platform and examined it carefully. When he had concluded his scrutiny he turned to the camera and tripod. He next went over the floor, section by section. All this took more than twenty minutes and I must confess my heart sank as the time passed without his discovering anything out of the ordinary.

He straightened up eventually and dusted the knees of his trousers. I was surprised to see an expression of alert excitement on his features.

"This does not bode well, Pons?"

"On the contrary, it tells me everything, Parker."

He moved over to the heavy wooden easel which stood in one corner. There was no canvas on it and I would not have given it a second glance. But as Pons grasped it he gave an exclamation of satisfaction.

"As I suspected, Parker. The whole thing is fastened to the floor."

"To the floor, Pons?"

"Yes, Parker. If I am not much mistaken it is used as a lever. Just hold the torch will you and stand close by me."

I took the flashlight from him and steadied it up on the wooden structure. Pons bent to it with a grunt. His hands moved about, seeking a purchase, and then he had thrown his whole weight against it as though it were a point-lever in a railway signal cabin.

"There is a counter-weight, evidently," he said thoughtfully as there came a perceptible rumble. I was so startled that I almost dropped the torch when a black hole suddenly appeared in the flooring of the platform, growing longer until it reached almost to my feet.

"Brilliantly ingenious," said Solar Pons, taking the torch from me and casting its beam down the stairwell.

"As you will see the boarding was not tongue and groove up here, but fitted flush. It was the only possible explanation to the mystery."

I now saw that the heavy pine planks of the floor had separated to form steps; they were held from beneath by flat pieces of metal screwed to them and which from below I had taken as strengthening bands for the ceiling. The whole thing resembled nothing so much as a gigantic piece of trellis-work.

"But why all this elaboration, Pons?"

"Supposing some of Mr. Schneider's lady-friends were illustrious names, who could not afford a scandal, Parker. What simpler than the pretence of renting a garage in this quiet spot. The lady could simply drive her car in, lock the door behind her and ascend to the studio from the interior of the store-room and no one the wiser."

I gazed at Pons in mute admiration.

"You are undoubtedly right. You knew this all the time, Pons!"

Solar Pons slowly shook his head.

"I knew there had to be an entrance. The motive for it did not cross my mind until we found those letters in Schneider's study."

He put his hand on my arm, his head on one side.

"Have your revolver ready, friend Parker. Something is moving in the garage below. I fancy I have just heard the outer door softly close. Take no chances but if you have to shoot try to wound rather than kill. I will just get to the light-switch yonder."

He moved silently away, extinguishing the torch. I had the revolver in my hand when the staircase trembled to a furious tread and a gigantic shadow rushed toward me in the bleached moonlight.

7

There was a savage cry which made my nerves jump but my hand was steady enough as I levelled the revolver. The huge figure reached the top of the stairs and turned toward me with incredible speed, the heavy mass of timber held threateningly over its head.

"For heaven's sake, man!"

Pons' voice, crisp and incisive, rang out as there came the click of the light-switch and the studio was bathed in incandescence. I stood as though paralysed but I came to myself at Pons' cry.

"Fire for your life, Parker!"

The vast man with the yellow face distorted with hatred was almost on me when I squeezed the trigger. He grunted and turned aside, scarlet spreading on his shoulder. I jumped back to the edge of the platform as he fell with a crash, the heavy billet of wood flying from his hands. Pons was beside me in a flash, pinning the fallen giant.

"Help me with this rope, Parker. A flesh wound only, I fancy, but he will be formidable indeed when he recovers from the shock."

I swiftly helped him to pinion our prisoner's hands and when we had secured him, I urged him up with the revolver. The heavy yellow face was sullen, the eyes burning viciously with pain and anger.

"Take no chances, Parker," said Pons coolly. "If he tries anything further shoot him in the leg."

The Chinese, who was dressed in blue chauffeur's livery, with white gloves, turned to Pons.

"I no understand."

"I think you understand well enough," said Pons equably.

He helped the groaning man into an armchair which stood just below the platform. He crossed over to me to take the revolver.

"Now, Parker. Your department, I think."

He covered the Chinese while I made a rapid examination and roughly bandaged the wound with my handkerchief. I pressed it back and bound it with an old trunk strap I found in the corner of the room.

"A flesh wound only, Pons. It has gone right through."

Pons smiled slightly.

"You have been fortunate, my friend. Dr. Parker here is an

excellent shot. Though I fear you have been spared merely to provide work for the hangman."

The chauffeur shook his head stubbornly.

"I no understand. I see light. Think burglars."

Solar Pons' smile widened.

"I think not. It really will not do. This man is undoubtedly the murderer of Romane Schneider, Parker. Though obviously the tool of others."

"I do not understand, Pons."

"You will in due course, Parker. We are nearly at the end of the road. But here, for a start, is the big man we were looking for."

"He is certainly that, Pons."

"Is he not?"

Solar Pons had a mocking smile on his face.

"We will just have a few words with his employer."

"His employer, Pons?"

"Certainly. Colonel Gantley."

I stared at Pons in puzzlement.

"Come, Parker. It does not take very much reasoning. This is Colonel Gantley's chauffeur and general factotum or I will give up my title to whatever reputation my modest talents have earned me."

"But what has Colonel Gantley to do with this, Pons?"

"Everything, Parker. He pays £100 a week for Cheneys, as a start. And by the time we have crossed the strip of lawn which separates this studio from the house, I shall no doubt have thought up a few more questions for him."

He prodded the bound giant to his feet. With me following behind we descended the outer stairs of the studio and picked our way through the garden to where the lights of the Colonel's house burned dimly before us.

A dark-clad servant answered Pons' insistent ringing at the bell and stared in disbelief at the bloodstained form of the groaning chauffeur.

"Kindly announce us to your master," commanded Solar Pons.

As the man still stood there Pons pushed him aside unceremoniously.

"On second thoughts we will announce ourselves. Where is the Colonel?"

"In the drawing room, sir," the man stammered.

But our dramatic entrance had already been heard and before we were halfway across the luxuriously appointed hallway with its hanging brass lantern, a mahogany door on the far side opened and Colonel Gantley came out, his hair shining silver in the lamplight.

"What is the meaning of this outrageous violation of privacy, sir?"

"It means, Colonel Gantley, that your little charade is over. Unless you wish the entire household to hear, I advise that we adjourn somewhere private to talk."

The Colonel's face was suffused with rage as he took in the state of the chauffeur.

"Chang! What have you been up to?"

Then a shock passed across his face. It was cleverly done but I could have sworn he was acting.

"Why, it's Mr. Pons, is it not? We met this morning."

"You would have a short memory indeed, Colonel, if you had forgotten already."

The Colonel was leading the way into the drawing room. A tall, dark man who was sitting near the fireplace with a glass of brandy in his hand made as though to jump to his feet but the

Colonel signalled to him with a lowering of the eyelids and he relaxed on to the divan again.

"This is my associate, Mr. Belding."

Solar Pons inclined his head curtly and turned back to our reluctant host.

"You will be pleased to hear that we have found the man responsible for the death of Romane Schneider, colonel. Your chauffeur here."

Colonel Gantley gasped and took a step toward the big Chinese, who stood with impassive, if pain-wracked, features.

"Romane Schneider? Murdered? How terrible!"

"I said nothing about a murder, Colonel," said Pons blandly. "Though I see you know all about it. Remarkable in view of the fact that we mentioned only a burglary."

The Colonel's face went ashen and he made a choking noise. The man by the fireplace leapt up but I already had my revolver out.

"I think not," said Solar Pons gently. "Dr. Parker here is a crack shot and we have already had enough violence for one evening. If you have a weapon in your inside pocket there, Mr. Belding, I sincerely advise you to drop it."

Colonel Gantley's forehead was beaded with sweat and he seemed to sag suddenly.

"Do as Mr. Pons says," he advised his colleague.

"Pray collect it, Parker. I will look after these two. Now, Colonel Gantley, I urge you to make a clean breast of things. You are already an accessory to murder and the other charges I will proffer should assure you at least twenty years in prison. It is in your interest to co-operate."

I took the heavy calibre pistol from the dark-haired man and motioned him over to join Gantley and the Chinese on a divan at the other side of the fireplace. Gantley sank into the cushions and passed a handkerchief over his face.

"I see it is useless to dissemble, Mr. Pons. Just what exactly do you know?"

"That is better, Colonel Gantley," said Solar Pons crisply. "When there is truth between us, we may progress. If you assist the authorities in this matter, they may be inclined toward leniency. Otherwise, I can promise nothing."

A groan trickled out from beneath Gantley's tight-pressed fingers.

"You are right, Mr. Pons. I did know about Schneider's murder. But I want you to believe I had nothing to do with it; it was not ordered by me and I was appalled and horrified when I learned what Chang had done."

Solar Pons' expression was grim and stern as he looked down at the abject figure of the Colonel.

"I am inclined to believe you. And it may be that you have been more of a dupe than anything else, though there is little excuse for you. You have been engaged in a foul and inhuman trade and must take the consequences."

"I do not understand you, Pons," I began, when my friend silenced me with a gesture.

"You must realise, Colonel Gantley," he went on, "I can promise nothing, though my recommendation to the police authorities might carry some weight if I were able to present them with a watertight case."

We were interrupted at that moment by a loud rapping at the door.

"Are you all right, Colonel? Do you wish me to call the police, sir?"

"Certainly not!"

The Colonel's voice was a strangled squawk and Solar Pons gave me a thin smile as the Colonel hurried over toward the door. I noticed that Pons remained close behind him while I kept my pistol trained upon the second man before me. There was a muffled colloquy at the door and then Gantley was back.

"I will tell you everything. I hardly know where to begin, Mr. Pons."

"Let me tell you what I have learned, Colonel. Then you can fill in the missing pieces."

"Very well, sir."

Solar Pons went over to stand at a point midway between the two men. He made a subtle gesture to me with the thin fingers of his left hand and so I continued to cover the dark man, Belding. The chauffeur, Chang, sat silent and impassive, nursing his wound, his face white despite his yellow pigmentation. His eyes burned vindictively into mine.

Solar Pons faced me in a contemplative mood and began to speak to me as though we were alone at 7B Praed Street.

"There were two baffling mysteries about this case, Parker. The murder of Romane Schneider in a sealed room and the lack of motive. You now know how the murderer gained access."

"But I still do not know why, Pons."

"Precisely, Parker. I shall proceed to tell you if I am allowed freedom from interruption. The puzzle in the sealed room was the method of entry and exit. There had to be one because the murderer could not just vanish into thin air. He had also to be a huge man, as I had already demonstrated, because Romane Schneider was about six feet tall and had been hit squarely upon the crown of the head with shattering force. As the skylight, the obviously solid walls and the main door were ruled out for the reasons we have already discussed, there remained only the flooring.

"I had already noticed from the building below that it would have been impossible for anyone to have gained entry from the garage as it had a solid cement ceiling. That left only the store-room and a number of interesting possibilities emerged. There were various buttresses and pillars which, to my mind, ruled out a staircase in that portion of the building. It had to be a staircase or ladder because of the height of the studio from the ground. There was only one possible place and I immediately saw that it corresponded with the position of the raised platform in the studio above."

Solar Pons paused and looked at the crushed form of Colonel Gantley with glittering eyes. The man Belding held himself coiled tightly like a spring but I held the revolver ready and the expression on my face evidently deterred him.

"You may recall that I paid particular attention to the studio flooring, Parker. And that I found traces of the murderer which petered out near the foot of the shallow stairs leading to the platform. That merely reinforced my suspicions and I soon saw that though the floor was apparently solid, there were faint cracks between the pine planking at various points, instead of the tongue and groove joints which obtained elsewhere. I was convinced that an entrance would be found there and so it proved. We then had the problem of why the staircase existed and who had used it.

"I had only to see Godfrey Horrabin and Sir Hercules Kron-feld to eliminate them from my inquiries. Though both physically fitted the requirements it was obvious, from the frank and open way in which he answered my questions and my reading of his character, that Horrabin would not have destroyed his own livelihood as the dead man's secretary. Similarly, Kronfeld was genuinely moved at his old enemy's death; as I observed, there was a similar love-hate relationship between Gilbert and Sullivan. Sir Hercules had been a personal friend until the two men quarrelled; in my opinion the feud between the two men, real or supposed, added salt to life for both.

"Two vital pieces of information emerged from my examination of Schneider's study, both of which had been overlooked by Jamison. Or rather, no proper conclusions had been drawn from them. The existence of the staircase which led only to the store-room and garage was far more plausible when it became clear that the dead sculptor was a notorious womaniser. Discretion was assured when a woman had only to drive her car into the garage, using a key supplied by Schneider, and gain access to the studio secretly and privately by using the staircase.

"Though we have not had time to find it, there is obviously a button or some mechanism down below which operates the thing from the store-room. The motive for the crime was supplied by my finding among Schneider's papers that Colonel Gantley here was paying the incredible sum of £100 a week for the privilege of renting Cheneys. It would have to be a profitable antique business indeed which could support such an outlay."

Colonel Gantley gave another groan and turned a haggard face toward Pons.

"Shall I tell you why Colonel Gantley paid Schneider £100 a week, Parker?"

I nodded.

"Because so much money was being made by the Colonel and his associates that money was no object. There were certain pressures on them and they had to get a respectable address with storage facilities immediately."

Colonel Gantley spoke.

"The police had just raided our headquarters in Limehouse, Mr. Pons. I had instructions from above to evacuate all our supplies from Deptford. I brought them here just in time."

Solar Pons started tamping tobacco into the bowl of his pipe.

"I suspected something of the sort. I remembered the newspaper reports a short while ago. And my suspicions became aroused when I saw the crates which had come from such places as Hong Kong and other cities in the Far East."

"I wish I knew what you were talking about, Pons," I protested.

"Tut, Parker, it was a simple deduction," said Solar Pons, lighting his pipe. "Following the murder some of the crates had been hastily moved and part of the contents spilled. You may remember I tasted some white powder which was on the floor. As a doctor, Parker, the implications should have been obvious."

"Drugs, Pons!"

"Of course, my dear fellow. Cocaine and opium, mainly, I should imagine. Hong Kong is one of the great clearing houses for the trade in the Far East. Furthermore, all the crates we saw were marked with red stars. I felt certain in my mind that these would be sure to contain genuine antiques or souvenirs. Colonel Gantley here was only a tool, part of a large ring. I have a shrewd suspicion who was at the centre of the web."

"I beg of you, Mr. Pons," said Gantley, in a shaking voice. He looked quickly at Belding, bit his lip and turned away again.

"But what has all this to do with the murder, Pons?"

"Everything, Parker. Let us just reconstruct the matter. Romane Schneider was in financial difficulties, we already know. He decided to let his house and rent a less expensive one. He was naturally delighted when Colonel Gantley turned up at the estate agents and made his extravagant offer. But may we not conjecture that after some weeks of tenancy, his curiosity got the better of him? Why was an antique dealer like Colonel Gantley, a man with a relatively modest income, so keen to pay £100 a week?

"Why did he store so many things from the Far East inside the rooms below the studio? And why did he employ Chinese almost exclusively among his outside staff? That was so, was it not, Colonel Gantley?"

"You are guessing, Mr. Pons, I imagine. But you are right, yes. A number of Chinese have been here. I have told my superiors about it, but these men are experts at the trade. Mr. Belding was their supervisor."

"You fool!"

Belding had sprung up with a white face before I could stop him and struck the Colonel in the mouth. I caught the dark man across the skull with the barrel of my pistol and he dropped noiselessly on to the divan.

"Well done, Parker," said Pons drily. "I see that your reflexes have lost nothing of their hair-trigger reaction. You had best examine him. I do not think we need fear trouble from Colonel Gantley."

I gave the dark man a cursory examination while Pons took the pistol and covered the chauffeur.

"He will be out for half an hour, Pons," I said.

"Excellent. That should be time enough. Where was I? Ah, yes, Romane Schneider's fatal curiosity. As the months went by the movements and actions of his intriguing neighbours aroused his suspicions. Two nights ago he stayed in his studio after dark, keeping all the lights off.

"When he judged it was safe, he let down the staircase. I submit he had already looked through the store-room window and noted that there were no crates in the area beneath. He crept down in the dark and made a thorough examination. What he discovered we shall never know. But the contents of the warehouse were so vitally important that the intruder could not be allowed to live. Or that was the reasoning of this man here."

Pons looked thoughtfully at the sullen Chinese.

"I fancy we shall hear nothing from his own lips. He is certainly inscrutable enough for that, though there is enough circumstantial evidence to ensure him the hangman's rope. Schneider was in the store-room when he heard a sound. It might have been the Colonel's car returning. At any rate Schneider, thoroughly frightened, ran back up the staircase and regained the studio.

"He dared not return the staircase to its original position because of the noise. He decided on boldness. He put on the light in his studio as though he had just come in and started work on one of his sculptures. Unfortunately for him the Chinese must have seen the light shining down through the staircase and went to investigate. He saw at once how things were and being a man of action took the decision into his own hands to eliminate Schneider.

"He crept quietly up the staircase—perhaps under cover of the car engine he had left running below—and struck Schneider down from behind with his own mallet. He then retreated to the ground floor and informed the Colonel of his action."

"Brilliant, Pons." I said.

"It is a reconstruction only, Parker," returned Solar Pons. "We shall need the Colonel's verification."

"It is correct in every detail, Mr. Pons," said Colonel Gantley, looking at my companion with something like awe. He had a handkerchief to his face and staunched the blood from his cut lip.

"Of course, my horror at the crime can be imagined, but it was all too late. We made a thorough search of the store-room and found a small lever at floor level which operates the staircase from below. After I had made an examination of the studio and made sure there was nothing incriminating left behind, we put the stairs back, left the lights on and piled up crates and boxes to ceiling level. We spent another hour in removing the remaining drugs to the cellar of this house."

"You did admirably well under the circumstances," said Solar Pons ironically. "I am sure you will correct any details in which I have gone wrong."

Colonel Gantley shook his head.

"I have only myself to blame, Mr. Pons. Easy money was my downfall, as it has been for so many others. I had been cashiered from the Indian Army. I returned to the old country but nothing I touched prospered. I started an antique business but that was foundering. I was desperate for ready money when I met Belding in a public-house one evening about a year ago.

"He told me of a way I could make money and I slowly became enmeshed. My business, which had legitimate contacts in the East, was useful, you see, and the men behind the trade found I provided a respectable façade. There is no excuse for me, I know; I have helped to ruin countless lives—and now this."

"There is one way you can redeem yourself," said Solar Pons, a stern look upon his features. "The names and addresses of every contact and as many men as possible higher up in the organisation."

Gantley shook his head.

"Belding was my only major contact. And the Chinese we employed. I will give what help I can."

"Be sure that you do."

Solar Pons stood deep in thought for a moment, pulling gently at the lobe of his left ear, while a thin column of blue smoke ascended from his pipe to the ceiling.

"It was too much to hope for, Parker. As I said before, the trembling of the web, but the spider remains concealed in the shadow."

"You surely do not mean your old enemy, Pons?" I cried.

"It is possible, Parker. No crime is too despicable for that scoundrel. And he would need such enormous profits as that generated by the drugs trade to fuel his infamous criminal empire. Just ring Jamison, will you? We must make sure he has not inadvertently arrested Sir Hercules or Schneider's unfortunate secretary."

8

"It was a remarkable case, Pons."

"Was it not, Parker?"

We were at lunch in our comfortable sitting-room at 7B Praed Street a week later and Mrs. Johnson had just brought the midday post up. It was a beautiful June day and the window curtains stirred gently in the cooling breeze. Pons chuckled and passed me a copy of the *Daily Telegraph*. I found a large item on the front page ringed ready for cutting out and pasting into the book in which he kept records of his cases.

"Jamison has excelled himself. At least one drugs ring has been smashed and a stop put to the traffic in that quarter. Belding himself led to some of those higher up. It was more than might have been hoped for."

"Thanks to you, Pons."

Solar Pons smiled wryly.

"Ah, Parker, you were ever generous in your evaluation of my work. In my humble way I seek to alleviate some of the ills of mankind."

"You have certainly done a good deal here, Pons," I said.

Solar Pons shook his head.

"It is just plugging holes in the dyke, Parker. There is such great profit in this foul trade that it is almost impossible to stamp out. One does what one can. My major satisfaction in this particular case is that Baron Ennesford Kroll has been robbed of considerable profit in the matter. You will see that Heathfield, through Jamison, has made a clean sweep of the Limehouse area, and now that Gantley, Belding and the Chinese are going for trial, this will mean a considerable, if temporary, setback, in the Baron's plans."

"I do not see how you can be so sure about the Baron's part in this, Pons?"

"One develops a sixth sense, Parker. Hullo. Here is something interesting. Postmarked Switzerland, I see."

He tore open the thin blue envelope which Mrs. Johnson had just brought up with the other letters. He studied it in silence, his eyes narrowed. Then he put it down with a low chuckle.

"Talk of the devil, Parker."

"What is it, Pons?"

By way of an answer he passed the single sheet of paper the envelope contained across to me. It bore just two lines, written in block capitals with a thin-nibbed pen.

MR. PONS—YOUR ROUND, I THINK.
WE SHALL MEET AGAIN.

K.

Solar Pons sat back at the table and lit his pipe.

"He is the most dangerous man in Europe, Parker. I would give a great deal to have netted him."

And his eyes looked beyond the homely commons of our room and gazed bleakly into the void.

THE ADVENTURE OF THE
SURREY SADIST

1

IT WAS A wet, mild day in early April, and I had made my rounds in a somewhat irascible temper, not aided by my own discomfort and the streaming colds of many of my patients. I finished early, and as my evening surgery was being taken by my locum, I returned to the comfortable living quarters I shared with my friend Solar Pons at 7B Praed Street in a somewhat more amiable frame of mind.

There was a low fire in the fireplace, and when I had poked it up, I sat by it, looking vacantly at the flames and savouring the first few sips of the welcome hot tea provided by the ever-thoughtful Mrs. Johnson. I was sitting so, lost in a twilight reverie, when there came a lithe step on the stairs, and the door burst open to admit the lean, athletic form of Pons.

Raindrops were gleaming on his cape, and his alert, clear-minted features were alive with suppressed excitement. He threw off his heavy garment and laid it over a chair, rubbing his thin hands together.

"It is certainly murder, my dear fellow," he observed. "Do I see fresh tea there? If so, I will join you."

"By all means, Pons," I said, shifting my position to enable my friend to get closer to the fire. "Allow me to pour you a cup."

Pons sat in silence until I had passed him the tea and then sank back in his armchair, his eyes closed.

"I take it you were not referring to the weather, Pons," I observed.

"Eh, Parker?"

Pons opened his eyes and leaned forward toward the fire.

"You mentioned murder."

"Oh, yes, Parker. It is certainly that. An end will be put to the activities of Tompkins, the well-known grocer of Shoreditch, once my report is in."

I smiled at my companion and got up to ring for Mrs. Johnson. Our amiable landlady had promised to bring more tea and more substantial fare once Pons had returned. In fact, no sooner was my hand off the bell when I heard her measured tread on the stair and hurried to open the door for her. She put the things down on the occasional table near the fire and took the cover off the hot, buttered crumpets.

"You have excelled yourself, Mrs. Johnson," said Pons appreciatively.

The good-humoured features of Mrs. Johnson relaxed in a broad smile.

"Good of you to say so, Mr. Pons," she murmured. "Have you yet seen the gentleman?"

"What gentleman, Mrs. Johnson?"

"The gentleman who called here an hour ago, Mr. Pons. He left his card with me. I thought you might have run into him in the street, as I saw him pacing up and down half an hour or so ago."

Solar Pons stroked his chin.

"Let us just hope he returns, Parker. London has been too dull of late. Have you the card, Mrs. Johnson?"

"I have it here, Mr. Pons."

My companion took the card from Mrs. Johnson and studied it for a moment or so. Then he passed it to me.

"Be so good as to give me your opinion, Parker. Thank you, Mrs. Johnson. If the gentleman returns, you may show him up."

"Very well, Mr. Pons."

Our landlady withdrew and left us to our agreeable meal. I glanced at the card. It was a large and expensive one with gilt script printing. It said: EMIL RAWNSLEY COLEFAX. And underneath, the address: CLARENDON COURT, OXHILL, SURREY. I handed it back to Pons.

"A gentleman of taste and discernment, evidently. Well-to-do and with a gracious home."

"You excel yourself, Parker. Anything else?"

He passed the card back and I turned it over.

"Nothing that I can think of, Pons. Oh, yes, there is something written here."

I studied the microscopic writing in the right-hand corner.

"Must consult urgently. Utmost importance. E.R.C."

Solar Pons rubbed his hands together briskly.

"This sounds promising, Pons."

"Does it not, Parker? Anything else?"

I shook my head.

"An elderly man, perhaps. And one obviously tended by a large number of servants, judging by his address."

Solar Pons' eyes positively sparkled.

"Excellent, Parker. You are constantly improving. But I fear that you have overreached yourself in some of your conclusions."

"Where have I gone wrong, Pons?"

"In a few details only. Contrary to your suppositions, I think we shall find that our client is a young, vigorous man, certainly not over forty. He will not have servants and will probably live quite frugally. While he has a good address, he has not a lot of money to spare. And though young and strong, he currently is terrified."

I stared at Pons open-mouthed and then from him to the card.

"And you have concluded all this from a study of the card?"

"That, combined with a lifetime's intensive usage of the ratiocinative processes, Parker."

"You must admit the card is an expensive one, Pons."

Solar Pons nodded and ate the last morsel of crumpet before wiping his lips with his handkerchief.

"I give you that, Parker."

"And the address is an expensive one also."

Solar Pons inclined his head.

"Possibly. But not quite so lavish as you imagine. If I mistake not, the Clarendon Court is a large private hotel or a block of flats. I have the advantage over you, you see, for I saw an advertisement relating to the very place only a few days ago. Just hand me that bundle of *Telegraph*s, will you."

I passed him the journals in question from the side table and waited while he glanced through them.

"Ah, here we are. Well-appointed residential hotel in quiet, secluded surroundings."

He handed me the item.

"So you see, Parker, there goes your estate and large retinue of servants."

I made a wry mouth but persisted nevertheless.

"But a young and vigorous man, Pons."

"I have made some considerable study of handwriting, Parker. You will see from the writing that the strokes are firm and vigorous. The hand is certainly that of a young man. The clinching factor is that no elderly man, who might be enfeebled, would pen a message in such microscopic writing but at the same time so legibly."

"You may be right, Pons."

"I am sure I am, Parker. When we combine these factors with the information that our man has been hanging about the street for half an hour or more on such a wet day, the image of an elderly man disappears altogether."

"You mentioned he was terrified, Pons. You deduced that from the message, of course."

Solar Pons shook his head.

"Not at all. But the firmness of the strokes wavers here and there. Here, if you will look at the card again, the nib of the pen has penetrated right through the heavy card. Agitation, Parker. Combined with the message it gives us a young man suffering from stress."

"But the frugality and lack of money."

Solar Pons smiled briefly.

"I was chancing my arm a little there, Parker, but I will be surprised if it is not so. Do you not see the difference in the lettering?"

I studied the card again.

"The gilt of the man's name seems to be a slightly different colour from that of the address, Pons."

Solar Pons slapped his knee with a cracking noise.

"Capital, Parker! Our potential client has had a stamp of his name made. He could not afford to have such expensive cards

141

printed for himself. So he merely prints over the heavily embossed cards of the hotel."

I threw up my hands.

"I shall have to give up duelling with you, Pons!"

Solar Pons smiled amiably.

"Not at all, Parker. Though I must confess my little jousts with you prevent the reasoning faculties from atrophying altogether."

He turned as there came a ringing of the front doorbell.

"Ah, there, if I am not mistaken, is our client now."

The man Mrs. Johnson ushered into our presence a few moments later was indeed, as Pons had surmised, a thin, sensitive-faced person of about thirty-eight years old. Pons could not resist a quiet smile in my direction as he rose to greet our guest.

"Mr. Colefax, of course. I am Solar Pons, and this is my friend and colleague, Dr. Lyndon Parker."

"Delighted to meet you, gentlemen."

"Will you not remove your coat before you sit down?"

The young man bit his lip and flushed. He shrugged deeper into the garment and sat on the edge of an easy chair I had pulled over for him.

"I think not, Mr. Pons, if you don't mind. I am chilled to the bone."

"As you please."

Again the swift, penetrating glance from Pons' deep-set eyes. Our client, now that I had a good look at him, was neatly but rather shabbily dressed. His overcoat, though of good quality and cut, had seen better days, and I could see that his shoes were much scratched and worn, the laces broken and retied. Once again I marvelled at the incredible penetration of Pons' keenly honed mind.

Solar Pons leaned back in his chair and commenced to light his pipe, his eyes never leaving our visitor's face.

"Would you care for some tea?"

"Thank you, no, Mr. Pons. I do not eat before eight o'clock in the evening."

"You are in some trouble, I understand."

Colefax, who had fair hair and a frank, open face, compressed his lips and nodded.

"I will not beat about the bush, Mr. Pons. I fear for my sanity, if not my life. You will hardly believe my story."

Solar Pons leaned forward and threw his spent match into the fireplace.

"You must just try me, Mr. Colefax. You would not credit the bizarre tales that have been told me in this sitting room, eh, Parker?"

"Most decidedly, Pons."

Our client leaned forward and put his two hands together in front of him, working his thin fingers together restlessly.

"I am of a very nervous and sensitive disposition, Mr. Pons. When a child, I was subject to what were then called nervous fits, and I suffered much from depression and bouts of melancholy. I come from a good but somewhat unstable family. My parents and I did not get on very well, I am afraid."

"It is often so in such cases," I reassured him. "I would not worry about it too much if I were you."

"But I do worry about it, doctor," said Colefax earnestly. "The discord between myself and my parents got worse as I became older. It culminated in a terrible row over a young lady to whom I became engaged. The engagement was broken off as a result. I became bitter and never forgave my father."

Our visitor paused, and an awkward silence fell until Pons nodded to Colefax to resume.

"Another bone of contention was my choice of career. I wished to become a commercial artist. I had some talent in that direction, but my father, who was a distinguished architect and wealthy in his own right, forbade it. Instead, he apprenticed me to a firm of architects."

The young man looked up with suddenly trembling hands.

"You must find all this terribly boring, Mr. Pons," he said apologetically.

Solar Pons shook his head.

"On the contrary, it is extremely revealing, Mr. Colefax. Pray continue and tell us your story in your own way."

Relief showed on the young man's face as he resumed.

"Despite my apparent falling-in with my father's wishes, there was continual friction at home. Again, I became fond of a young lady and again, because of parental pressure, the association was broken off. There were more rows, and eventually I left home. My mother died soon afterward. I had one stern, unforgiving message from my father. He had cut me out of his will just as he had now cut me out of his life. As you can imagine, I was extremely upset, principally because of my mother, who had been fond of me in a somewhat austere way. Even I had not known the depths of my father's hatred of me and of my way of life."

"Come, Mr. Colefax," I protested. "You do yourself an injustice, surely."

Our client shook his head.

"It is good of you to say so, doctor, but I felt the fault must lie within myself somehow. I was an only child, you see, and both my parents expected so much of me. I had disappointed my father in so many ways."

"Even so, your parents had shown extreme selfishness, if you will forgive me for saying so," said Solar Pons suddenly, sending a cloud of aromatic blue smoke up to the ceiling as he took the pipe from his mouth. "They had opposed not only your choice of career but your choice of wife, not once but on several occasions."

"That is true, Mr. Pons," said our client in subdued tones. "But I could not see it that way. I had a nervous breakdown after the receipt of my father's message and was unable to work for some time. Indeed, one might say I am still suffering both from the physical and financial effects of that period. But eventually I got work as a commercial illustrator in Oxhill, Surrey, and managed to keep afloat. I live very modestly at a private hotel and am tolerably comfortable, though I have to watch my pennies, as I have precious few savings."

He paused again with an embarrassed air.

"This was the situation that existed for some years. Then I read in a newspaper a few months ago that my father had died. It was another shock to me, of course, as I had heard nothing from him. I saw from the published figures of his will that he had left a fortune in excess of two hundred thousand pounds."

I looked at our client with an astonished face.

"You did not hear from his lawyers or receive any approach from them?"

Colefax shook his head.

"No, doctor. There was no reason why I should. I was more concerned with my father. Though he had treated me badly, I was still fond of him and had hoped for reconciliation. In any event, there was no way anyone could have contacted me, as I had lost touch."

Solar Pons shook his head.

"Even so, there are ways in which they could have traced you," he said. "The money does not concern you? I hope you do not wish me to take up any legal claim for you."

Colefax looked at my companion in astonishment.

"Good heavens, no, Mr. Pons. It is nothing like that. I am in deep trouble and do not know where to turn. I have little money but..."

Solar Pons raised his hand with a soothing gesture.

"Say no more, Mr. Colefax. It is just that putting claims to lawyers is hardly in my line. Mine is a criminal practice and concerned, so far as is possible, with the righting of wrongs."

Colefax was silent for a moment, and his haggard face looked pitiful in the dim light of our sitting room, the firelight only emphasising the deep hollows under the eyes. He looked at me quickly.

"You do not think I am mad, doctor?"

"I?"

I looked at him in surprise.

"My dear fellow, why should I?"

Colefax passed a shaking hand over his forehead.

"My parents have been much on my mind for years, I know. They are both dead, as I have told you. Yet I have seen them both as clearly as I see you, within the past two weeks!"

2

Solar Pons tented his thin fingers together in front of him and stared at our visitor with very bright eyes.

"This is extremely interesting, Mr. Colefax. You are highly strung, as I can see for myself, but despite your extraordinary statement, I see no reason to doubt your sanity."

Young Colefax flushed, and a weary smile flitted across his face.

"It is good of you, gentlemen. I am glad to have your reassurance. The shock of this business has been unnerving, I can tell you."

"Just tell me about it," said Solar Pons.

"Well, Mr. Pons, the Clarendon Court is a tall, rambling old building set in well-wooded grounds. It obviously was once a country estate. I occupy a small side room. It is not ideal, but it is all I could afford. There is not much of a view. In fact the room, which is on the first floor, looks out onto a whitewashed wall of a garage block, with gloomy rhododendrons nearby. I had come back from my work one night about a fortnight ago. I put on the light and went to draw the curtains, when I was transfixed, Mr. Pons. Staring at me from near the bushes outside was the figure of my mother!"

Our visitor paused, evidently overcome, and Pons leaned forward to scrape the bowl of his pipe with a small metal instrument he kept for that purpose.

"That would be enough to unnerve anyone, Mr. Colefax. Please describe the circumstances most particularly. Where was she standing, for example?"

"Against the garage wall, near the rhododendrons, Mr. Pons. She was motionless for a few moments. I am afraid I gave a great cry, the sight was such a shock to me, and the figure immediately disappeared. I rushed outside, of course, but there was nothing there. On top of that, Mr. Pons, I got a torch and searched around carefully. Where the figure of my mother had been standing was a freshly dug flower bed. There was no sign of any footprints or that the soil had been disturbed."

"If it were a ghost, you would not expect to find footprints," mused Solar Pons. "Yet your search was invaluable, for it proves—at least on the surface—that someone masquerading as your mother could not have been responsible, for the soft earth would have retained the impression of shoes. How was this figure dressed?"

"That is another strange thing, which upset me a good deal, Mr. Pons. My mother was as I remembered her in childhood. Young and dressed in old-fashioned clothing with a large picture hat."

"Hmm."

Solar Pons tamped fresh tobacco into his pipe and leaned back in his chair, lost in a reverie.

"What happened next?" he said at length.

"The next evening, the figure of my father appeared in the same place."

I stared at our visitor.

"This is extraordinary, Pons!"

"Is it not, Parker? How was he dressed?"

"That is bizarre also, Mr. Pons. It is as though my memory had been recalling them from childhood. Father was much younger and dressed in the style of thirty or so years ago."

Pons knotted his brows, frowning at the young man through his pipe smoke.

"The late Victorian age. Does not that suggest something, Parker?"

I shook my head.

"It may to you, Pons. It means nothing to me, I am afraid."

"Well, no matter. You again investigated, I take it?"

"Certainly, Mr. Pons. I ran out at once, but the figure had already gone. Again, there had been no disturbance in the flower bed."

"Was the figure standing in the same place?"

"A little farther along the wall, Mr. Pons."

"It did not move at all?"

Colefax shook his head.

"No, Mr. Pons. Both figures just stared at me, as though reproachfully. What does it mean, Mr. Pons?"

There was a brief silence before my companion replied.

"Something sinister, Mr. Colefax. I have no doubt of your sanity. You have seen these figures again?"

"Yes, sir. On three occasions in the past ten days. In all, I saw my mother twice and my father three times."

"By day or by night?"

"By night, Mr. Pons. I had got to look for them, you see."

Solar Pons pulled at the lobe of his right ear and looked at me sombrely.

"Each time you ran out, and each time there was nothing there?"

"Yes, Mr. Pons."

"No one else saw the figures?"

Our client hesitated.

"I did not ask anyone, Mr. Pons. It is a quiet place in front of my bedroom window, in any case, and hardly anyone goes there. Besides, in view of my past medical history, I did not like to draw attention to myself in that way. It is easy to become labelled as an eccentric in such an enclosed world as a hotel, and I am comfortable enough there and should not like to move."

"Quite so."

Solar Pons smoked on in silence for a few more moments.

"Tell me about the occasions when you did not see the apparitions, Mr. Colefax."

149

Our client looked startled.

"Let me see, now. There were two nights when it was foggy. So I would not have seen the figures in any case. And there was a heavy rainstorm one evening."

Solar Pons removed the pipe from his mouth.

"That accounts for eight nights out of the fourteen, Mr. Colefax."

"I spent last weekend away with friends. The other three or four nights my nerves were so bad, I kept the curtains tightly drawn."

Solar Pons nodded.

"I see. Have you seen a doctor?"

Again our client flushed—again the same uneasy shifting in the chair.

"I did consult my doctor after the first two appearances, Mr. Pons. I did not, of course, tell him anything about the figures I had seen. I merely said I was suffering from nerves. He found nothing wrong with me physically."

"I see."

Solar Pons continued to stare at our visitor through the wreathing clouds of smoke.

"You were extremely agitated when you left the card. And you have been pacing the street for a considerable time. Something else has happened."

Colefax turned a haggard face toward my companion.

"I was in bed last night, Mr. Pons. I had not dared look out of the window. It was very late, and I was still awake when I heard stealthy footsteps in the corridor. Something was slipped under my door. I rose, put on the light, and found an envelope. I have it here."

He passed an ordinary white envelope to Pons. The latter

turned it over and extracted a small sheet of paper from it. He studied it in silence, then glanced back to our client.

"You have done well to come to me, Mr. Colefax. This is extremely grave. Pray give me your opinion, Parker."

He passed the sheet across. It bore only a few lines in crabbed, rather faded handwriting. The bottom part of the paper had been cut rather clumsily. The message read:

> Punishment does not extend only to this life but to the afterlife also. And it is retrospective. You have got to be made to realise that, Emil. Your actions are abhorrent to your mother and myself. Justice will prevail.

"Good heavens, Pons!" I exclaimed. "What does this extraordinary message mean?"

Young Colefax's lips were trembling and his face white as he replied.

"Retribution from beyond the grave, Dr. Parker. That is my father's handwriting!"

3

Solar Pons was the first to break the silence.

"As I have remarked previously on more than one occasion, this agency stands four-square behind the natural laws of physics, Mr. Colefax. I do not believe in ghosts, and Parker and I, together with occasional assistance from the doctor's revolver, have disproved them in a number of cases. I will not comment on what my colleague calls, quite correctly, this extraordinary message, though I understand what a shock to thenerves this sinister business must be. I will take the case, of course."

"Mr. Pons!"

Our client rose impulsively and wrung my companion's hand effusively. Solar Pons relinquished the other's grasp with a thin smile.

"We have not yet solved this mystery, Mr. Colefax. Reserve any thanks due until the conclusion of the case. I have still to finish my questions."

"I beg your pardon, Mr. Pons. What else can I add?"

"You saw no one at the door?"

Colefax shook his head.

"I opened it immediately, before I looked in the envelope, but there was no one there. The corridor turns at right angles just beyond my room, in any event."

Solar Pons wrinkled his brow again and puffed furiously at his pipe.

"Did you ever hear any strange noises in the hotel? Or outside? Just before or just after these strange appearances and disappearances?"

Colefax puckered up his lips.

"Nothing out of the ordinary. I remember a small tapping noise at the window just before I first saw the figure of my mother on the grounds. I thought it was a branch against the pane. The trees grow rather close just there."

"Very well."

Solar Pons sat very still, his intent eyes never leaving the young man's face.

"Anything else?"

Colefax shook his head.

"Nothing other than the ordinary noises of the hotel. Distant coughs, footsteps passing the room occasionally, windows opening and closing as guests leave or return to their rooms."

"I see. Have you any other relatives?"

"Nobody really close, Mr. Pons. There is only my uncle, Mr. Edward Colefax. He is my father's brother, but I have not seen him for years. He lives at Eastbourne. My family came from there."

"Indeed."

Solar Pons sat silently for a moment or two longer.

"Have you a photograph of your parents as they were in recent years?"

"Certainly, Mr. Pons. I have one in my wallet here."

He produced it and passed it to Pons, who in turn handed it to me. I studied the two grave-faced elderly people, who stood stiffly on the porch of an imposing country house, as though posing for a Victorian photograph.

"Does your uncle resemble your father?"

"Oh, no, Mr. Pons. As you see, my father had a mane of thick grey hair. Uncle Edward was taller, thinner, and quite bald."

"He is younger, I take it?"

"Oh, yes, Mr. Pons. Some fifteen years or so."

"Good. That will be all, Mr. Colefax, unless you have anything startling to add. We shall be with you by late afternoon tomorrow. Tell no one at the hotel that we are arriving, and in fact we must appear to be only casual acquaintances. Are you free to accompany me, Parker?"

"I should like to, Pons. I will just telephone my colleague."

"Excellent. And pack your revolver. We may have need of it."

Colefax's eyes were big and round in his face.

"What do you suspect, Mr. Pons? Is there any danger?"

Solar Pons smiled reassuringly.

"There may be, Mr. Colefax. I would prefer to be on my guard. As for yourself, do not look out your windows or investigate any noises you hear in the night. We have something more tangible to fear than ghosts, I should imagine. Keep your door locked and your eyes open."

Colefax licked his lips and looked at Pons apprehensively.

"You could not come down tonight, Mr. Pons?"

Solar Pons shook his head.

"I have a few inquiries to make tomorrow morning, which can only be done in town. The information may be vital, and it is necessary that I arrive on the grounds armed with all possible facts."

He put his hand on our client's shoulder.

"I do not think you are in any immediate danger, Mr. Colefax. But there is no time to lose. Follow my instructions, and you will be quite safe for one night. If you would be good enough to show our visitor down, Parker. Good-night."

4

Solar Pons was out most of the morning the following day, which had dawned more bright and cheerful, and he came back to 7B at about twelve, briskly rubbing his hands together.

"We progress, Parker, we progress."

I gazed at him in astonishment.

"You mean about young Colefax?"

Pons nodded.

"I am on the way to establishing a motive. It will largely depend on the guests at the hotel, I fear. I hope you have your overnight things handy, for we leave on the four o'clock train."

"I wish I knew what you were talking about, Pons," I remarked irritably.

Solar Pons laid a thin forefinger along his nose.

"All in good time, my dear fellow. Are those chops I can smell grilling down below? Mrs. Johnson is excelling herself these days."

"I told her we were going into the country for a day or two, and she evidently thought we might not be well fed there."

Solar Pons smiled thinly.

"Did she not? Mrs. Johnson is ever thoughtful for our welfare, Parker."

He turned and looked out of the window.

"I just have to make one telephone call and pack, and I shall be free to face the rigors of Surrey. At least it is no longer raining today."

As he spoke, a watery sun gilded the panes of our windows. He crossed over to his favourite armchair and sat cross-legged, facing me.

"What do you make of this business, Parker? Let us just have your views on the matter."

"The appearance of these figures is quite inexplicable, Pons," I began cautiously.

"Is it not?"

"And then there is the important detail of the flower bed. If the soil has not been disturbed, then I cannot see that anyone could have been standing there."

"I am glad to hear you say so, Parker. Excellent reasoning. Had there been footprints, my theories would have received a considerable knock."

"This is a quite impenetrable mystery, Pons."

"Oh, come, Parker, do not say so. The combination is quite

irresistible. We have a young man—nervous, tense, subject to depression and breakdowns—one-time heir to a considerable fortune, who sees the phantom figures of his dead mother and father. And when the father writes to him in an unmistakable hand, that should give one an inkling of which way the wind blows."

I stared at Pons with considerable irritation.

"You are making sport of me again, Pons."

"On the contrary, my dear fellow. You did not fail to notice, of course, that the sheet of paper bearing the father's message had been cut with a pair of blunt scissors?"

I choked down my rising choler.

"Really, Pons! The paper was too long for the envelope, obviously. When cut in half, it was easier to fold in two."

"Of course," said Solar Pons languidly. "I am delighted to see such logical reasoning in the afterlife. But I fail to see why a ghost would need scissors at all, let alone a blunt pair."

I maintained a dignified silence and sat down immersed in *The Times* until lunchtime. Pons was busy in the early afternoon and disappeared for a short while, presumably to make his call. We got a cab to Waterloo and shortly after five o'clock found ourselves on the platform of the main station at the bustling market town of Oxhill, the spire of a misty grey cathedral rising from the cluster of red roofs before us.

It was a market day, and it took a while for our taxi to thread through the narrow streets and the main square, which was thronged with shoppers, who swarmed about the long lines of market stalls with striped awnings. We drove out of the town for about a mile, over sandy, undulating uplands clad with pine and fir. The sun was staining the distant hills a dazzling red, and I was lulled into a comfortable somnolence, which was broken by a muttered observation from my companion.

"It is a remarkable paradox that some of the vilest crimes take place not in the squalor of mean streets such as that found in the capital, but against the deceptive and so-called beauty of nature."

"Really, Pons," I protested. "I see only the charm of Surrey. As the poet remarked, 'Only man is vile'."

"*Touché*, Parker," said Pons gently, the sunset gilding his lean features a pale bronze. "A palpable touch. You are constantly bringing me to a sense of my own limitations."

I smiled.

"Hardly that, Pons. But perhaps I act as a necessary corrective."

"It might well be, my dear fellow. The driver appears to have brought us by the most direct route, for here surely is the Clarendon Court."

🖉 5

We drove through a stone-pillared entrance gate up a gravel drive between gracious lawns to the large, red-roofed building, surrounded by ancient trees. A white board screwed to a post indicated the name of the hotel in black italic letters, and a grey squirrel scampered across the lawn as our vehicle drew up near a line of cars that were parked outside the hotel. There was a warm glow from within, and the noise of a string quartet came to us from a long, mullion-windowed tea room almost opposite. I got out and stood appreciatively sniffing the aroma of the pines.

"Come along, Parker," said Pons with a thin smile. "You will get bronchitis standing there."

"I am the physician, Pons," I protested. "And Surrey is noted for its health-giving atmosphere."

"It is also extremely damp this afternoon," said Pons casually, putting down his valise and walking back along the façade of the building. He waited until the taxi had disappeared down the drive before leading the way toward a block of red brick garages that stood to one side, set amid heavy clumps of rhododendron.

"This must be the place of which young Colefax spoke, Pons."

"The fact had not escaped me, Parker," said Solar Pons gravely.

He stepped round the end of the garage and followed it along. The bricks of the garage wall there had been painted white, no doubt to alleviate the sombre shadow cast by huge clumps of rhododendron, which soared more than thirty feet high in this spot. Pons had stopped now and was looking carefully at a larger flower bed, about six feet wide and some fifteen feet long, which fronted the garage wall.

"There has certainly been no one walking on this bed, Parker," said Solar Pons. "Unless he has afterwards carefully raked the soil."

He looked at me quizzically.

"But then I should have been extremely surprised had there been any traces."

"I do not follow you, Pons."

"No matter, Parker. Things will clear as we progress."

He stepped back and looked at the façade of the hotel opposite.

"The garage wall is about twenty feet from the window of Colefax's room, wouldn't you say, Parker?"

He pointed to the large sash window, almost directly opposite, on the first floor. I nodded assent, glancing upward to see that there was a line of windows above our client's room, extending upward to the whole four storys of the rambling old building.

"It seems a very extensive property, Pons."

Solar Pons stroked his chin.

"They knew how to live in those days, Parker, when ancient families ran such houses. Servants were cheap and the economy stable. A little different from these bustling days."

Pons stood deep in thought for a few moments longer, but I knew the sharp eyes and the keen brain were noting and evaluating data the importance of which was hidden from me. He suddenly gave a brief exclamation and turned away.

"I think we have seen enough here. Let us just register and unpack."

The hotel was indeed a comfortable and spacious place and seemed to be well patronised. We were given cheerful rooms on the first floor, overlooking the spacious lawns, and when we had made a hurried toilet, we descended to the tea room, where a four-piece orchestra of a surprisingly high quality was heavily engaged in a selection of Viennese waltzes.

To our surprise, I saw our client sitting two tables away, with tea things on the table before him, engaged in conversation with a tall, dark-haired man who was leaning over the table, evidently having just come from a nearby seat. I was about to make a remark to Pons when he forestalled me.

"I have already seen him, Parker," he observed drily in a low voice.

"What say you to toasted teacakes and scones with strawberry jam, my dear fellow?" he added loudly, as the waitress had just paused at our table.

I gave the order and when we had settled to the tea, looking casually about the large, oak-beamed room, which was fairly crowded, I noticed that the tall man had finished his conversation with Colefax. He passed quite close to us, and I saw that he was an amiable-looking person, expensively dressed and with good taste.

"I am surprised that Colefax is not at his work today, Pons," I said.

"I asked him to be available for our purposes, Parker," said Pons. "Now that we are here, I wish you to keep your eyes open. I have a notion that one of our young friend's fellow guests might have some intention of doing him harm."

"Good heavens, Pons!" I mumbled, my mouth half-full of teacake. "You cannot mean it, surely. Do you mean to say someone here might have dressed up to impersonate Colefax's father and frighten him like that? But what is the purpose?"

Solar Pons smiled, his keen eyes stabbing round the room.

"Not so fast with your theories, friend Parker. You will only confuse yourself. Just absorb what I have already said, and take careful note of what you see about you."

Colefax had already left the room when we finished tea, and after a brief stroll in the gathering dusk, Pons and I returned indoors. There was no one about in the long, broad corridors as we went to our rooms. To my surprise Pons, instead of turning left, took me right, down an unfamiliar corridor.

"Number fourteen, I think," he said, glancing at a door we were passing.

"I will just look round this corner. Hmm. As Colefax told us, the corridor turns at right angles."

We walked up to the second floor, and Pons spent a good deal of time looking at the room numbers, before he expressed himself satisfied. I had watched these activities with mounting bewilder-

ment but said nothing, and now Pons again led the way downward, pausing to rap cautiously on the door of Number 14.

Colefax opened the door quickly, his eyes sparkling with
excitement, and he closed it softly behind us.

"Thank you for your promptness, gentlemen. I feel much
better already now that you are both here."

"I am glad to hear it," said Solar Pons with a reassuring smile,
looking rapidly around the room.

It was a small, comfortable chamber but somewhat gloomy,
and even at this time of the evening, Colefax had the light on.
Pons crossed to the window and stood looking down at the
gloomy vista of the rhododendrons and the garage wall, grey
now in the fading light.

"That is where you saw the apparitions?"

"Yes, Mr. Pons. Exactly there. The position varied by only a
few feet on each occasion."

"Within the fifteen or so feet of the flower bed, in other
words."

"Yes, Mr. Pons."

"Hmm."

Solar Pons was again silent, the fingers of his right hand
plucking at the lobe of his ear. Then he leaned forward and slid
the window sash up. He looked out and craned his neck upward
to examine the façade of the building above. Young Colefax
watched him in obvious puzzlement.

"The figures were life size on each occasion?"

"Of course, Mr. Pons. As one would expect."

"Naturally, Mr. Colefax. As one would expect."

Pons was absorbed for a few moments, pacing the room,
stopping now and again to examine something that caught his
interest.

"Who was the gentleman with whom you were talking at tea?"

"Merely a hotel acquaintance, Mr. Pons. Mr. Poynter, I think his name is. He has been here some weeks. I understand he is a manufacturer from the Midlands who is currently resting for his health."

"I see."

Pons moved toward the door.

"Well, Mr. Colefax, just remember what I have said and be on your guard. We are in Rooms twenty-four and twenty-five, just down the corridor, if you should require us urgently. We will in any event see you at dinner."

"Very well, Mr. Pons. And thank you both again."

When we had left the room and were walking back down the corridor, my attention was arrested by a sudden scratching noise. I turned to see a large, bearded man regarding me curiously. He was standing a little farther on from our client's room and inserting his key into the door lock. It was obvious, to my mind, that he was making a clumsy attempt at being occupied, while observing us closely.

I caught my companion by the arm as we hurried on.

"Did you see that, Pons? The bearded man? His behaviour looks highly suspicious to me. And the beard itself does not look genuine, to my mind."

Solar Pons chuckled.

"You may well be right, Parker. Why did you not give it a tug to make sure?"

I looked at Pons indignantly.

"You may laugh, Pons, but I am convinced the thing is not genuine. I may well take you up on your remark if we see him again."

Solar Pons was still smiling as we descended the main staircase toward the reception area.

"Well, it will do no harm if we can obtain the gentleman's name without arousing suspicion. An old acquaintance, perhaps? Room number sixteen if I mistake not."

And he walked over toward the girl behind the reception desk, and I soon saw that they were engaged in deep conversation, the register being consulted from time to time. When Pons rejoined me, he was rubbing his thin hands together with satisfaction.

"Mr. Nicodemus Serafis, Parker. From Bulgaria, I believe."

I snorted with indignation.

"An entirely implausible name, Pons. Most likely completely fictitious."

"It does seem rather unlikely," said Pons mildly. "I also took the opportunity to glance down the register for the past few weeks. We have a number of other unlikely semi-permanent residents, I regret to say. We shall have to use our eyes and ears."

He glanced at his watch.

"Now, we just have time for a quick trip into Oxhill before dinner, Parker."

I looked at him in surprise.

"Oxhill, Pons?"

"Yes. I have a fancy to visit one or two local photographers."

"Photographers, Pons?"

"Certainly. We are tourists, are we not? Would you be good enough to order a taxi, my dear fellow?"

"But surely they will not be open at this time of day, Pons. It is almost six o'clock."

Solar Pons' expression was pained.

"You disappoint me, Parker. Enthusiasm is the watchword. If the premises are closed, surely it will not be too difficult to press the bell at those establishments where the owners live above the shop."

"If it is important enough, Pons."

"It is certainly that. But it is my recollection that even in provincial towns, such shops will not be closed before seven or eight o'clock."

He strode toward the front of the hotel.

"And after dinner tonight, we must be sure to retire to the main bar, Parker. Hotel bars are great hotbeds of gossip, and we may learn something to our advantage there."

6

"This affair seems more baffling than ever, Pons."

"Do not say so, Parker. We have made considerable progress this evening."

Solar Pons rubbed his thin hands together, his deep-set eyes sparkling as he surveyed the people in the crowded bar through the haze of blue smoke. We sat in an angle of the brick inglenook fireplace, in comfortable leather chairs, our glasses on the small oak table in front of us.

We had made our expedition into Oxhill, a charming town of red brick houses with the occasional oak-beamed medieval structure converted into shop or antique dealer's premises that one finds in that part of Surrey. Pons had drawn a blank at two photographic establishments. But at the third, which was still open and whose bearded owner was an enthusiastic master of his craft, Pons had begun an erudite conversation on the merits of $f2.5$ lenses and optical focusing that had ended with the proprietor strewing the counter with the latest examples of photographic equipment.

He had seemed equally indifferent to commercial considera-
tion and did not seem to mind whether Pons bought anything
or not. Eventually the conversation had drifted onto the subject
of lantern slides, on which Pons' new friend seemed to be equally
expert, and I became completely lost. Eventually I excused
myself and went to wait in a nearby tea shop, where Pons eventually joined me, his lean, feral features ablaze with satisfaction.

Now he appeared strangely content and parried my few questions about the results of our visit to Oxhill, though he seemed
lively enough on other subjects.

When Colefax's acquaintance Poynter passed through the bar,
Pons evinced little interest in him, being more intent upon the
bearded man Nicodemus Serafis, who was deep in conversation
with a little, thin, rat-faced man in a salt-and-pepper suit, in a
small cubby-hole on the other side of the fireplace.

Eventually Pons turned to me, a thin smile curling his lips.

"Are you still of the same mind, Parker?"

"Regarding Serafis, Pons? His actions and attitude remain
suspicious to me."

Solar Pons chuckled.

"Do they not? And yet the man with whom he is talking,
Solomon Tappenden, is one of the most respected Hatton
Garden diamond merchants."

"You surprise me, Pons. How could you possibly know that?"

"Oh, there is nothing remarkable about it, Parker. He
registered in his correct name, as any such merchant would do,
trusting to the obscurity of the venue."

"I do not follow you, Pons."

"I fear it would not be the first time, Parker. I would hazard
that they are doing business together."

"Then there is something sinister behind it, Pons."

"My dear fellow, if you will insist on reading more into things than are apparent on the surface, you do poor justice to my training."

"I do not trust that bearded fellow, Pons. I would hazard a guess that he might well have something to do with this weird business of young Colefax. And that beard appears damnably false to me."

Solar Pons gave me a wry look.

"I see there is no putting you off, Parker. Very well. You must just put your theories to the test."

I stared at Pons for a long moment.

"I am inclined to take you up on it, Pons."

"That must be your own responsibility. I do not know Tappenden by sight, but I know the name, and it is a most respected one. Moreover, a small leather bag has passed between them, which under the circumstances could only contain diamonds."

"I was not talking of Tappenden, Pons, but of his companion, Serafis."

My friend shrugged.

"There is nothing unusual about diamond merchants wishing to do their business out of town. Such hotels as this are popular venues for quite enormous transactions. Dealers such as Tappenden often do not wish others in the market to know what is in the wind."

"I have no doubt Tappenden is honest, Pons," I said. "It is Serafis whose character does not seem to sit right."

Solar Pons chuckled.

"Come, Parker. There is no time like the present, and we must not let such a valuable theory of yours go to waste."

And he rose, draining his glass, and led the way through the crowded bar passing directly by the two men's table. I made as if to follow, and when I got opposite them I pretended to stumble. I do not know what I quite intended, but I received a nasty shock.

As I went down, I put out my hand and caught hold of the dark man's beard. Instead of it coming off in my grasp, as I expected, Serafis gave a howl of pain and rage, tears springing to his eyes. I sprang back from him with a mumbled apology. The whole bar fell silent, and I could see Solar Pons' mobile features in the background. He was having some difficulty keeping a solemn countenance.

"Really, sir!" the bearded man spluttered. "This is an outrage. I will protest to the management."

"Please accept my apologies, sir," I mumbled. "It was entirely an accident."

Somehow I stumbled away and found myself in the hall of the hotel, conscious of the repressed mirth in Solar Pons' eyes.

"Well, Parker," said he. "I hope you are satisfied. Action without closely rationalising one's theories can be entirely too dangerous sometimes. You had better walk around to the other bar and have something strong to settle your nerves."

And he tactfully led the way while I recovered myself.

7

"Now, Parker," said Solar Pons. "Just pay close attention, for we may have a strenuous period ahead of us."

We were sitting in a small side bar of the hotel, sipping whiskies and sodas, and my nerves had indeed recovered from my little contretemps, as Pons had predicted.

Our client, Colefax, had entered half an hour earlier but,

pursuant to Pons' instructions, had taken little or no notice of us. He had been joined a few minutes later by Mr. Jervis Poynter, the Midland manufacturer, who nodded affably and struck up a desultory conversation. The two men had a drink and then left the bar together. To my surprise, Solar Pons was on his feet, draining the remains of the whiskey in his glass. He looked over at the old cased clock in the corner of the bar.

"Almost ten o'clock and a dark night. Time to be moving, I think. Conditions are ideal, and our man must press home his advantage if he is to win through. Fortunately, he does not know we are on the grounds."

"What on earth are we going to do, Pons?"

Solar Pons laid his finger on his lips.

"We will just join young Colefax in his room and await the turn of events."

He led the way out of the bar back into the main hallway and loitered, pretending to examine a poster advertising a forthcoming carnival dance in the locality, while Colefax and Poynter, absorbed in conversation, climbed the stairs. When we reached the familiar corridor, the two men were saying good-night at the door of Colefax's room.

We waited until the door had closed behind our client and the tread of Poynter had died out along the staircase as he ascended to his own chamber. I was about to make some remark to Pons, when a heavy footstep sounded along the corridor, and the scowling, bearded face of Serafis was thrust back over his shoulder. The key grated in the lock of his door farther down the corridor, and then there was silence.

Solar Pons, with a dry chuckle, led the way to Colefax's room and rapped softly on the panel. We were admitted immediately, and Pons at once sat down on the edge of the bed, motioning to me to be silent.

"We have not long to wait this evening, I think," he whispered. "It is a dark, dry night, and he will not delay until you are in bed."

"Really, Pons," I began. "If only you would . . . "

"Hush, Parker."

Solar Pons put his hand on my arm and motioned me down into an armchair near the window.

"If you will just switch off the light, Mr. Colefax, it will assist matters, I think."

We waited for perhaps a quarter of an hour, and despite myself, an eerie sensation of premonition began to steal over me. As Pons had said, it was a fine, dry night, but some light stole in through the window blind, and occasionally a sharp gust of wind rattled the casement stealthily. All about us were the minute, everyday noises of a country hotel—the soft gurgling of water in pipes, the creaking of boards, footsteps in the corridors, the locking and unlocking of doors.

At last, when my patience was wearing thin, there came a heavy dragging noise from somewhere above. Pons was on his feet instantly, enjoining caution with a raised finger. At his gesture, Colefax went to stand by the window blind. I rose from my chair as a faint, insidious tapping began at the window. At almost the same moment, at a whispered instruction from Pons, Colefax threw up the window blind, making a great deal of noise in the process.

I could not resist a gasp of surprise, not untinged with fear. The night was dark, as we had noted, and there were few lit windows on this side of the hotel. The white wall of the garage opposite stood out indistinct and shimmering in the faint moonlight. Standing against the wall, on the flower bed, about halfway between two huge clumps of rhododendron, was the figure of a woman. A woman, moreover, who wore a large picture hat and the dark clothing of a bygone age. I turned at the sharp exclamation from young Colefax. He displayed a white, agitated face to us.

"Mr. Pons, explain it if you can, but that is my mother out there!"

Solar Pons put his hand on the other's shoulder.

"Do not distress yourself, Mr. Colefax. This business is almost over. Come, Parker! We have no tune to lose."

He led the way out of the room at a breathless pace, and I was hard put to it to keep up with him as we hurried up the thickly carpeted staircase. Pons led the way unhesitatingly to one of the doors on the outer side of the long corridor. He quietly tried the handle.

"This is no time to stand on ceremony, Parker. We must break it down."

I looked at him silently for a moment. Then we ran at it together. The lock gave with a rending crash, and we were within a darkened room, lit only by a beam of light. An indistinct figure crouching by the open window gave a muffled curse, and then Solar Pons was at the light switch.

Jervis Poynter blinked in the strong light and then came at me with a snarl. I had not forgotten my old boxing skills and dropped him with a right hook. He hit the floor with a crash and rolled over, unconscious. Solar Pons hurried forward, his eyes dancing with pleasure.

"Well done, Parker! That will hold this pretty rascal for a while."

He bent down and pulled at the thick hair. The wig came away to reveal the bald cranium of a middle-aged man.

"Allow me to introduce you to Mr. Edward Colefax, our client's uncle and one of the most cold-blooded villains who has ever walked in shoe leather."

"You cannot mean it, Pons!"

Solar Pons lit his pipe, shovelling out clouds of blue smoke over his shoulder as he looked down at the recumbent figure before him.

"I do mean it, Parker. He was the only possible person. It was fairly evident from the start what was behind these apparitions that plagued young Colefax, and it was only a question of establishing the link and the method. The motive was fairly straightforward."

My amazement must have shown on my face.

"You knew all this before ever we came to Surrey, Pons?"

"Let us say I suspected it, Parker. Proving it was another matter."

There was a noise at the door, and the agitated face of young Colefax appeared. He looked stupefied as he gazed at the unconscious figure of his uncle.

"Who is this, Mr. Pons?"

"The man who has been persecuting you, Mr. Colefax. The man whom you knew as Jervis Poynter, but who was in reality your own uncle, Edward Colefax, carrying on an elaborate masquerade."

Colefax gasped and would have fallen if I had not supported him. I helped him to a chair.

"But for what purpose, Mr. Pons?"

"For the strongest of all motives, Mr. Colefax. Money. He hoped to drive you mad or to suicide and claim your inheritance."

"But I have no inheritance, Mr. Pons!"

Solar Pons slowly shook his head.

"You wrong your late parents, Mr. Colefax. But first allow me to demonstrate this piece of equipment, part of the deception and certainly valuable evidence. With the testimony of us three, it could secure your uncle a substantial term of imprisonment, should you care to prosecute."

Solar Pons stepped across the silent figure of the elder Colefax and bent over the bedside table. He threw a switch, and a strong beam of light shot from the metal instrument before him through the open window onto the garage wall. Once again I saw the ghostly figure of the woman in Victorian clothes. Colefax gasped.

"So that was how it was done, Mr. Pons. But how on earth..."

"All in good time," said Pons, holding up his hand. "If you would be so good as to attend your victim, Parker, perhaps Mr. Colefax would telephone for the local police. We should give this villain a good fright if nothing else. I then suggest we repair to the smoking lounge after hours, and I will throw even more illumination on this affair."

8

It was midnight. The police had been and gone, and Edward Colefax, a frightened and chastened man, had left on the late-night train. The evidence of which Pons had spoken reposed on the table before us. We sat in the comfortable panelled private lounge of the hotel, with a whisky decanter and soda bottle between us. A small fire of logs burned comfortably in the hearth and cast a ruddy glow on the faces of Pons and our client.

"I hardly know how to thank you, Mr. Pons."

Solar Pons chuckled, sending out a blue plume of smoke from his pipe.

"It was a fairly elementary matter, my dear sir, but not without some points of interest. As soon as I heard your story, I knew that no extraterrestrial phenomena were involved, and I immediately looked for an explanation as soon as I arrived on the ground. When I examined the garage with Dr. Parker here, I was already fairly certain of what I would find."

"And what was that, Mr. Pons?"

"You had already explained that there were no footprints on the freshly dug flower bed, so I directed my efforts to what would fit my preconceived theory."

"And what was that, Pons?"

"You will recall, Parker, that Mr. Colefax told us the apparitions of his parents did not appear regularly. There were certain evenings when they could not. Those were on nights of heavy rain or fog. I particularly asked my client about this, and it confirmed my suspicions. What I was looking for was a situation in which the figure could be projected to give the illusion that someone was standing against the wall, on the flower bed. And the figure had to be life size. That the images were motionless on all these occasions, but that their positions varied from time to time, only strengthened my theory."

"But what was the point of all this, Pons, apart from driving Mr. Colefax out of his mind?"

Solar Pons smiled thinly, tenting his bony fingers before him as he gazed into the heart of the fire.

"Patience, Parker. All in good time. I immediately saw that the wall was white, which gave an excellent projection surface; that there was a window above Mr. Colefax's, which would have done admirably from a projection point of view; that the twenty-foot distance would have been ideal if the right lens were used; and that the darkness of the great clumps of rhododendron that bordered the flower bed would provide shadow even if the hotel lights were on, which would ensure a clear image. As we have seen, friend Colefax was using a very powerful slide projector."

"So that was why you showed interest in the floor above Mr. Colefax's, Pons?"

"Exactly, Parker. Having ascertained that the room above our client's was number thirty-four, it was simple to check from the hotel register. That gave us the friendly Midlands manufacturer, Mr. Jervis Poynter. My theory was somewhat shaken at first because anyone more unlike Mr. Colefax's uncle it would be hard to imagine. I wanted a spare, bald man, and here we had a bulky man with thick hair. I soon saw, however, that Poynter's growth of hair could have been a skilfully made wig, and friend Parker here rapidly eliminated a suspicious-looking foreign gentleman with a beard, on whom my suspicions had briefly rested."

"You might have warned me, Pons," I grumbled.

Solar Pons smiled and shifted in his comfortable chair, reaching out for the whisky glass.

"I indicated the fact as forcibly as possible, Parker, but you were besotted with your own particular theory. Fools rush in . . ."

Colefax gave me a sympathetic smile.

"I am most grateful to you both. I have no doubt Dr. Parker acted for the best."

"No doubt," said Pons. "Having fastened on my man, I needed something a little more tangible to bring him to book. I visited a number of photographic dealers in Oxhill and soon found an enthusiastic man who was able to give me all the material I wanted. He had sold a powerful slide projector to a tall, bald-headed gentleman some while ago. The gentleman's name was Smith, of course, but the description fitted Mr. Colefax's uncle. Furthermore, he had made two slides up specially to his client's order. These were copies of pictures from an old photo album. Undoubtedly your parents, Mr. Colefax."

Pons took two photos from his wallet and handed them to Colefax.

"Why, Mr. Pons, they have been taken from my mother's album!"

Solar Pons nodded.

"Exactly. Colefax had to use those, as they were the only suitable pictures he had available. And being memories of your childhood, they would add to the terror the images would bring. We have that from your uncle's own lips."

Our client clenched his fists, an angry flush rising to his cheeks. Solar Pons leaned forward and put a reassuring hand on his arm.

"Compose yourself, Mr. Colefax. It is all over now. In addition, your uncle purchased a special lens that made the images he wished to project on the wall exactly life size. As you will see here, he had the slides made up specially, with clear glass all round, which would show only the figure and prevent a square picture shape on the wall."

"It was a damnably clever scheme, Pons," I said, picking up one of the slides.

"Was it not, Parker? And it might well have succeeded had not Mr. Colefax consulted us. The uncle attracted his victim's attention by lowering an ordinary cotton reel on a length of twine from the window above, which he used to tap on the glass. When he heard the blinds drawn, he immediately switched on the lantern, waited until the image had time to register on our client's mind, and then switched it off. He had spent some time adjusting the machine on the table in his room so that the image was always sharp and clear when he switched it on."

"Clever, as you say, Pons, but I am still not quite certain about all this. Why did he go to the photographic dealer's in his own persona?"

"To avoid identification with the fictitious Mr. Poynter when he walked about Oxhill, of course. We are telling the story backwards, Parker, but it was as well to reassure Mr. Colefax conclusively of his sanity and well-being in the first instance. I am sure that as a doctor you would agree."

"Indeed, Pons. As I said before, you knew a good deal of this before you left London."

"I knew the motive, Parker. Never theorise without sufficient data. When Mr. Colefax told me about his parents' circumstances and his being cut out of the will, I remained doubtful. He had been estranged from them for some years and vowed never to take a penny, but there before us was the most powerful motive in the world. I went immediately to Somerset House and consulted a copy of the will. That was the reason I could not come to Surrey immediately, Mr. Colefax. I found that you were the sole beneficiary of your parents' estate."

Our client looked thunderstruck.

"You cannot mean it, Mr. Pons."

"I do mean it, Mr. Colefax. You are the possessor of nearly a quarter of a million pounds. Men would commit murder and worse to get that sort of money. Your uncle was no exception. There was a very important codicil in that interesting document. If you were to become insane or die prematurely, the bulk of the estate would pass to your uncle."

There was a long silence between the three of us, broken only by the falling of a log from the grate.

"Damnable villain indeed, Pons," I said. "I wish I had hit him harder."

Solar Pons chuckled.

"You did well enough, Parker. Here was the motive and force behind the entire elaborate scheme to drive the nephew mad. I then telephoned Mr. Colefax's house in Eastbourne. I was told that he was away from home for a month or so. To make doubly sure, I checked again from Oxhill yesterday. Colefax was still away. I felt certain he was here at the hotel, manipulating the strings of this devilish plot. Tell me, Mr. Colefax, did anyone in particular seek you out in the past few months?"

Colefax shook his head.

"No one, Mr. Pons. Except there was a very persistent salesman of encyclopaedias at the hotel here some two or three months ago. He tried to get me to take out a subscription and had filled in a form before I could get rid of him."

Solar Pons expelled a thick cloud of blue smoke.

"You gave him your correct name?"

"Certainly, Mr. Pons. There was no reason to hide it."

Solar Pons nodded.

"Well, there it is, Mr. Colefax. When you disappeared and Colefax eventually realised there might be a fortune for him in your parents' will if anything happened to you, he became desperately anxious to trace you. The lawyers could not do so, but they were rather half-hearted about it, as lawyers tend to be. They merely inserted advertisements in London newspapers, and naturally nothing came of it. I had that from them in person when I checked on the will and the codicil."

I stared at my companion.

"You had a busy morning, Pons."

"Did I not, Parker? But Colefax was more ingenious than that. It is not too difficult to find anyone in this country, providing he has not changed his name, and you had not done so. Colefax employed a private detective."

"The encyclopaedia salesman?"

"Exactly. And I will wager it was not long after his visit before Mr. Jervis Poynter took up his abode in the hotel."

"About a week, Mr. Pons, to the best of my recollection."

I could not resist a small stroke of mischief.

"And the note under the door, Pons?"

"That was elementary, Parker. It was obviously not written by Mr. Colefax's father. Or rather, it was written by him, but certainly not after death. It was an old diary entry in which an angered father expressed his private thoughts on the conduct of his son. We shall no doubt find that Colefax purloined it for his own purposes while going over the family property after his brother's death."

"You may be right, Pons."

Solar Pons stabbed the air with the stem of his pipe.

"I am undoubtedly right, Parker. The Oxhill police have already found the diary among this rascal's effects and have impounded it. The paper had been cut across to make it look like a note, with a rather blunt pair of scissors belonging to the hotel. That was what drew my attention to it."

"For what purpose, Pons?"

My companion looked at me pityingly.

"Because the following entry would not have squared with a note purporting to be a threat against the victim's life."

"I am still not certain of your meaning, Pons. But I am sure now it is over that Mr. Colefax would not wish to prosecute his own uncle."

"There is no choice, Parker. I told you the matter was one of life and death. Edward Colefax was determined to secure his brother's fortune at any cost. He did not shrink from attempting to drive his own nephew mad. If that had failed, he would have tried more drastic measures. The man was not only a sadist but a potential murderer."

Young Colefax's eyes were round with horror as he stared at Pons.

"You cannot mean it, Mr. Pons?"

Solar Pons gazed at the young man steadily.

"I was never more serious in my life. The police found a great number of things among Colefax's effects. An inspector with a warrant will be waiting to arrest him when he arrives at his home."

Solar Pons reached from the inside pocket of his coat and produced a small violet-coloured bottle.

"Just give me your professional opinion on this, Parker."

I uncorked the bottle cautiously and sniffed at the contents. I handed it back with a face that must have been as grim as my thoughts.

"Exactly, Parker," said Solar Pons with a visage of bronze. "I concur with your judgement. The contents undoubtedly include cyanide."

THE ADVENTURE OF THE
MISSING STUDENT

1

"GOOD MORNING, SOLAR!"

"Good morning, Bancroft!"

I looked up in surprise as the door to our comfortable sitting room at 7B Praed Street, which I shared with my friend Solar Pons, opened a trifle and was then flung wide open to admit the massive form of my companion's brother, Bancroft Pons.

"Things are slow at the Foreign Office, then, Bancroft."

"Tolerable, Solar, tolerable."

Bancroft Pons smiled enigmatically and sank into a comfortable armchair at his brother's side, bowing delicately to me as he did so, and tactfully ignoring the protesting squeaks of the springs at the unaccustomed weight.

"Would you care for some refreshment, Mr. Pons?"

"No thank you, doctor. This is a quick visit only."

Bancroft Pons looked around our sitting room with a twinkling eye. It was a warm, fragrant day in early May, and the grey aridity of London seemed transformed. The windows were open onto Praed Street, and it may have been my imagination, but I could have sworn there was a faint aroma of new-mown hay coming on the fresh breeze that blew in across the rooftops. I looked at Pons, aware that his lean, intent figure expressed heightened interest, even in repose.

"If you wish, I can leave you in private, Pons."

Solar Pons frowned.

"By no means, Parker. Unless my brother has any objection?"

Bancroft Pons shook his massive head.

"I am sure you have no secrets from Dr. Parker, Solar. I would be perfectly happy to have him present for our little talk."

"You have a problem, then?"

"Not I, Solar, not I. My neighbour in St. John's Wood. It is probably not worthy of your attention. But he seems rather upset. And I have no time for such matters, as you know."

Solar Pons tented his long, thin fingers together in front of him and looked with twinkling eyes at the portly form of his brother, who sat, heavy eyelids hooded, before him. He glanced across at me.

"You are free today, Parker?"

I nodded.

"My colleague is running the practice. It is my day off, which is why I am still reading the newspaper at ten o'clock in the morning. I had thought of running down to see an aunt in Tunbridge Wells this afternoon, but St. John's Wood will do just as well."

Solar Pons smiled thinly.

"Excellent, Parker."

"You have not yet heard the problem," said Bancroft Pons, with a malicious little smile.

"If you are here, Bancroft, it will be something unusual. For all your faults, you do not waste my time."

"Good of you to say so," Bancroft Pons murmured deprecatingly. "However, I will not bandy words. I have a neighbour, Silas Rillington, who lives just across the Crescent, at number twenty-seven. He has been plagued in the last two weeks by a number of mysterious and maddening incidents that have reduced him to a nervous wreck."

"Pray be more specific, Bancroft."

The heavy lids of Bancroft Pons' eyes lifted, and the pupils beneath regarded my companion sardonically.

"If you would allow me, Solar. Rillington is a retired merchant with connections in the East, who has been able to assist the Foreign Office from time to time in certain delicate negotiations. That is how I first came across him some years ago, and I was then surprised to learn that we were such close neighbours."

Bancroft leaned forward in his armchair, the springs creaking dangerously.

"He came across to see me yesterday evening. That was in itself unusual, as we never normally met at each other's homes, except by appointment. I had not seen him for some weeks, though on the last occasion I had noted he was rather pale. Last night I was shocked at the change in his appearance."

Bancroft Pons paused for a moment, but Solar Pons sat staring at him in silence until he was ready to resume.

"About a fortnight ago, he received a note written in block capitals, saying that if he wished to see his son alive again, he should leave, within three days, fifteen thousand pounds in used banknotes at the Charing Cross luggage-check office, in a brown paper parcel, addressed to 'Adam Bede'."

Pons smiled grimly.

"I take it he did not do so?"

Bancroft Pons shook his head. Before he could resume, I broke in.

"That is all very well, Pons, but how could the kidnapper, if such he be, retrieve such a parcel, as Mr. Rillington would retain the ticket?"

Solar Pons shook his head slowly.

"Come, Parker, it is the oldest trick in the world. The victim would be watched—the easiest thing to do in a great railway station, without the watcher himself being seen. He would note the size of the parcel, colour of paper, the ink used, and so forth, perhaps with the aid of an opera glass. Later in the day, he would come to collect the parcel, saying he had lost the ticket. Or he could merely ask for the packet addressed to 'Adam Bede'.

"There would be little danger, as he would probably be served by another member of the staff. But he would be able to describe the parcel, and there is no doubt it would be handed over to him."

"'Adam Bede' being a *nom de plume*, of course?"

Solar Pons' eyes held sparks of humour.

"It is more than that, Parker, being the name of a well-known novel by George Eliot."

Bancroft Pons had listened in disapproving silence to this exchange and could no longer restrain himself.

"If you would kindly let me finish, Solar."

"By all means, my dear fellow."

Somewhat mollified, Bancroft Pons shot me a stern glance.

"The affair is far more serious than that. As you say, Rillington did nothing about it. Foolishly, he tore the missive up and burned it."

Solar Pons made an irritated clicking noise with his tongue.

"The postmark?"

"He noted that. Central London."

"Good, Bancroft. That is something, at least. Why did he not contact the police?"

"He is reclusive and secretive, Solar. Pray let me finish. Two days after he should have delivered the parcel to the luggage-check office, he received a small packet by post. It contained a severed human finger."

I could not repress a shudder of horror.

"His son's?"

"The implication is there, Parker," said Solar Pons.

"He still did nothing?"

Bancroft Pons shook his head.

"Incredibly, no. It sounds unbelievable, I know, but he locked it in his safe. It had given him a considerable shock, however. The second and final blow fell yesterday."

"He received another packet?"

Bancroft Pons nodded.

"The first had contained the index finger of the right hand. The second contained the index finger of the left hand. The latter also included a brief note. It was chilling and to the point: UNLESS YOU DELIVER THE £15,000 BY WEDNESDAY, THERE WILL BE FURTHER DEVELOPMENTS."

Solar Pons frowned.

"Meaning that further portions of the son's anatomy would be amputated and parcelled up in a similar manner?"

Bancroft Pons gave his brother another disapproving look.

"Somewhat crudely put, Solar, but in essence, yes."

I could restrain myself no longer.

"What sort of father is it, Pons, that would ignore the help the police would give? To say nothing of parental feeling in the face of such horrific incidents?"

Bancroft Pons had a strange look in his eyes as he glanced across at my companion.

"That is just it, Solar. Silas Rillington has no son."

2

Our visitor could not restrain his expression of triumph as he gazed at the pair of us in the heavy silence that followed. Solar Pons smiled thinly and tented his lean fingers before him.

"You play your ace well, Bancroft, but I suspected something of the sort. You were a little too reticent on the subject of Rillington's son when you began your narrative."

There was a slight hint of disappointment on Bancroft Pons' face as he rose to take his leave.

"As Dr. Parker has so often remarked, Solar, there is no getting around you. I would be grateful if you could take the case. May I inform Rillington you will be able to stop by this afternoon?"

"By all means, Bancroft. And thank you for what promises to be an interesting commission."

"Think nothing of it."

And with a sardonic smile in my direction, Bancroft Pons glided surprisingly quietly from the room. When the street door below had closed, Solar Pons sat quietly for a few minutes, his keen eyes fixed vacantly on a spot near the ceiling in the far corner of the room.

"Well, well, Parker," said he after a while spent in this manner. "This sounds a pretty problem indeed."

"Bizarre and frightful, Pons."

My companion nodded.

"I shall have need of your medical knowledge, Parker. These severed fingers may tell us a good deal, if the right mind is applied to them."

I gave Solar Pons a long, steady glance.

"Does it not seem to you, Pons, that this neighbour of your brother's is a very strange person indeed?"

Solar Pons gave a curious smile as he took his pipe out of his mouth.

"Ah, you have noticed that, have you?"

"And this business of his son, Pons!" I burst out. "Or, rather, his not having a son."

"That tells us a good deal, Parker, does it not?"

"And then why did he not go to the police immediately?"

"Bancroft said he was reclusive, Parker. But you have a number of excellent points. I am glad to see that my little lectures on the importance of the ratiocinative processes have not been entirely lost."

Solar Pons rose from his chair and paced restlessly up and down the room.

"Today is Monday, Parker. Silas Rillington has until Wednesday to comply with the brutal request made in this latest note. But he has no son, as Bancroft has told us. Therefore, the solution is blindingly simple."

"It is far from simple to me, Pons."

"That is because you are not applying your mind in the right direction, Parker. Just hand me the *London Street Directory* and the *Commercial List* down from the shelf behind you, if you would be so good."

Pons took the two bulky volumes and browsed through them in silence until lunchtime. Afterward, we took a cab out to St. John's Wood, revelling in the clear, wine-like air and the agreeable and animated bustle of London in early spring. We alighted a quarter of a mile from our destination and walked the last stage, Pons smoking in silence, throwing out blue aromatic smoke in long plumes over his shoulder.

Silas Rillington's house proved to be a large white mansion set back on its own grounds and approached by a carriage drive. It was half-past two as we walked down the gravelled drive, and there were few people about, though birds kept up a cheerful warbling from the trees that were just bursting into green.

"Mr. Rillington appears to be a person of considerable wealth, Pons."

"Does he not, Parker? That is another significant factor that compels me to one conclusion only."

I stared at him but offered no comment, and a few moments later we rounded a curve in the drive and came out before the imposing entrance portico of the house. Approached by another spur of the drive was a large garage block, in front of which a liveried chauffeur was washing down a Daimler.

Our ring at the massive front door was answered by a neat parlourmaid. That we were expected was obvious, for we were immediately shown into the drawing room without further preamble. Despite the weather, a small fire of coal and wood was banked in the great stone fireplace, and the master of the house rose from a tall wing-back chair to greet us.

Silas Rillington was a thin, cadaverous man of medium height, with the deep yellow complexion often engendered by the tropics. He watched us with unwinking, bird-like eyes and extended an emaciated claw to Pons.

"You must excuse the fire, gentlemen, on such a spring day, but I have thin blood and am of advancing years. It was good of you to come."

"Not at all, Mr. Rillington," said Pons. "Allow me to introduce my friend and colleague, Dr. Lyndon Parker."

"You are most welcome, doctor. You may be able to shed some light on this dreadful business."

He gave an involuntary shudder, and his eyes jumped to a brown paper parcel on the table. The significance of this was not lost on Pons, who gave the table and then our host penetrating glances from his deep-set eyes.

"We have heard the salient facts from my brother, Bancroft Pons, Mr. Rillington. Is there anything you can usefully add?"

The old man waved us to chairs next the table and resumed his seat near the fire.

"Not a lot, gentlemen. I am a lifelong bachelor, so you can imagine that these references to my son in the notes meant nothing to me. But, of course, these loathsome enclosures were a great shock."

"Yet you did not call the police, Mr. Rillington?"

There was a curious, troubled look in the old man's eyes, and he hesitated a moment before replying.

"It seemed the work of some madman, Mr. Pons."

"Yet you had been threatened and ordered to hand over the considerable sum of fifteen thousand pounds? That is a police matter, surely?"

Again the curious look and the hesitation.

"In the ordinary event, Mr. Pons. That was why I consulted your brother."

"Yet a fortnight has passed since the first communication. During that time, someone's life may have been endangered—may well be forfeit. Have you stopped to think of that?"

Little spots of red burned on the old man's cheeks.

"I accept your implied criticism, Mr. Pons. But the man is still alive, obviously. Wednesday was mentioned in the latest communication, as you may see."

He indicated the bundle on the table, and Pons went over to examine it. I joined him and looked curiously at the two grim exhibits. They were the bloodstained, severed index fingers, as had been described.

"What do you make of them, Parker?"

"You will forgive me for not picking them up, Pons. Well-kept, sensitive fingers, obviously those of a gentleman. Not used to manual labour. Severed fairly recently, of course. A young man's hands."

"It is impossible to say exactly when they were severed? Or whether their owner was already dead?"

"Quite impossible at this stage, Pons," I said apologetically.

Solar Pons shot me an approving glance.

"Never mind, Parker. Your information is invaluable. I could have done no better myself."

"You are too kind, Pons."

My companion was already examining the packets in which the gruesome objects had come.

"This is a little more helpful, Parker. Careless, to say the least. Coarse brown paper, unusual twine—one of the fingers has been wrapped in an old copy of *The Lancet*."

I stared at Pons in surprise.

"You are not saying a doctor is responsible, Pons?"

Solar Pons had a thin smile on his face.

"It is possible, Parker. Doctors are not unknown to have performed criminal activities in the long catalogue of man's inhumanity to man."

He turned back to the parcels.

"Hmm. Both postmarked Charing Cross. Both fingers packed in newspaper and inserted into small cardboard boxes before being wrapped in brown paper. Addresses written with a broad-nibbed pen in the same hand."

"What about the message, Pons?"

I peered over my friend's shoulder.

UNLESS YOU DELIVER THE £15,000
BY WEDNESDAY THERE WILL BE
FURTHER DEVELOPMENTS.

"Block capitals, but the same pen, Pons."

"Is it not, Parker?"

Solar Pons wrapped the material back in brown paper.

"You have no objection to our taking charge of this, Mr. Rillington?"

The old man smiled bleakly.

"I, Mr. Pons? By no means. Let us hope that this is the last of all this."

"Let us hope so, Mr. Rillington."

Solar Pons stood bowed in thought for a moment or two.

"You were an Eastern merchant, I believe?"

"Correct, Mr. Pons. In Assam but also in China and Hong Kong."

"Exactly so. I understand that certain organisations in China have a nasty habit of sending such fingers to their intended victims?"

Our host's yellow face had turned white.

"I have heard so, Mr. Pons."

"I submit that this was the reason you did not wish the police called, Mr. Rillington."

Again, the angry spots of red were burning on the old man's cheeks.

"Let us say that you had run up against such an organisation in your time in the East, Mr. Rillington. The white man's ways are not always gentle, so far as his Oriental brothers are concerned. And the latter's organisations have a long arm. You feared that though they had made a mistake in the matter of your son, this might have been a threat of vengeance."

The old man half-rose from his chair, his face a mask of astonishment. I stared at Pons in bewilderment. A croaking noise came out of Rillington's mouth, and I hurried to loosen his collar.

"I shall be all right in a moment, doctor. Just give me one of those pills from the box in the drawer over there."

I did as he said and waited while the white faded from his face to be replaced by the yellow.

"I am sorry to have had to put it to you so bluntly, Mr. Rillington," said Solar Pons sombrely. "But we have so little time, and someone's life may be at stake."

"Well, I will say this, Mr. Pons," said the old man at last, fixing my companion with burning eyes. "One had sometimes to make harsh decisions when dealing with Orientals, especially in the world of big business, in which I moved. And it was big business, Mr. Pons. I made enemies and did things I later regretted. And it was at the back of my mind that those things were behind these parcels. They gave me a bad fright, I can tell you."

"I am glad you have been frank, Mr. Rillington. But you may set your mind at rest. There has obviously been a mistake. The man who kidnapped young Rillington is an amateur. He got the wrong Silas Rillington. Unless I miss my guess, we want Silas Rillington, the millionaire copper king."

The old man by the fireside gave a long, shuddering sigh of relief.

"You have lifted a great weight from my shoulders, Mr. Pons. Please send me your account without delay."

"I want nothing from you, Mr. Rillington," said Solar Pons curtly. "Your attitude may have cost a life in this affair. If you wish to make amends, drop the money into your nearest church missionary box. Good day to you, sir."

And he seized the parcel from the table and swept out so fast that I was hard put to keep up with him.

◈ 3

"**B**ut how on earth could you know, Pons?"

"Pshaw, it was elementary, Parker. It was obvious from the word go that there had been a mistake. I checked most thoroughly on the other Silas Rillington this morning. He has an office in Park Lane, a villa on Capri, and a network of business interests world-wide. He could afford ten times more than fifteen thousand pounds and regard it as petty cash. That in itself is significant, Parker."

"I must confess I am lost utterly, Pons."

We were in a taxi *en route* to the West End, and it was temporarily halted at the lower end of Regent Street when this conversation took place. Pons was silent until we reached our destination, looking with dark and sombre eyes on the brown paper parcel that lay on the seat between us.

We took the lift to the fourth floor of a luxuriously appointed suite of offices in the building of Rillington Enterprises. Pons still had the parcel clutched beneath his arm, and I looked at him in alarm.

"You are surely not going to tell him, Pons?"

"Good heavens, Parker, kindly give me credit for more tact."

And he enjoined caution by laying his finger alongside his nose.

"You certainly hit the target with the other Silas Rillington, Pons."

"Did I not? The purest guesswork, but I have made some study of tongs and Eastern secret societies. The old man's secretiveness in the face of such communications was so extraordinary that there had to be something dark behind it. You may rest assured that his conscience is far from clear so far as his own part in the running of our colonial empire is concerned."

I pursed my lips.

"It has often been so, Pons, I am afraid. Though whether they would do any better running their own affairs is another matter."

"You may well be right, Parker. But here we are. Would you please take my card in to Mr. Rillington?"

His latter remark was addressed to a severe-looking woman secretary in a dark, tailored suit.

"Mr. Rillington is extremely busy today."

"I am sure he will see me."

The woman's eyes widened as she glanced at the card.

"Very well, Mr. Pons."

We waited but a few moments before being admitted to the elegantly appointed office of the principal of Rillington Enterprises. A distinguished-looking man of about fifty, with a silver-grey moustache, rose from his desk to greet us. There was a query in his eyes as he glanced again at my companion's card.

"Mr. Solar Pons. And Dr. Lyndon Parker, is it not? This is an honour, gentlemen—though I am not quite sure how Rillington Enterprises can assist you. The metal industry does not seem quite in your line."

Pons smiled as he shook the other's hand and formally introduced me.

"You are perfectly correct, Mr. Rillington. I met your son some years ago, but I am afraid we have drifted out of touch. I was passing by here just now, and the name on the building jogged my memory. I wonder if I could trouble you for his address."

There was only polite interest on Silas Rillington's face.

"Rodney? I did not know you were acquainted, Mr. Pons."

"We met at a lecture some while ago," said Pons suavely. "I was most impressed with him. A very bright young man."

"He is that, Mr. Pons. I am only sorry he did not see fit to follow me in the business."

Solar Pons nodded, dropping into the chair indicated by Rillington. I sat down in a leather armchair at one side of the glass-topped desk and watched the two men in silence. As might have been expected, Pons was conducting the interview with great skill.

"He mentioned a particular interest, but I am afraid it escapes me at this distance in time, Mr. Rillington."

"Medicine. He is a student at Charing Cross Hospital."

Solar Pons' lean, feral face was alive with interest.

"Of course! Medicine. That was it. Is he living at home? Or I could call at the hospital if that were not convenient?"

Rillington was scribbling something on a sheet of mauve notepaper he had pulled across the desk.

"He is living away from home, Mr. Pons, though he is on the best of terms with his mother and me. He thought it better, and on reflection, I am inclined to agree with him. He tried the business, but it did not suit him. He is twenty-four now and well on with his studies, so we are glad to see him settled."

"So I should imagine. Have you seen him recently?"

Silas Rillington shook his head.

"Not for a month or so, Mr. Pons. But that is nothing unusual for Rodney. He is terribly erratic, I am afraid. We did have a message from the hospital some three weeks ago, though, to say he was going on holiday to Spain."

"He spoke to you himself?"

"No, my wife took the call. It was relayed through one of the hospital porters, I believe."

"And you have not heard from him since?"

"No, Mr. Pons."

Solar Pons looked disappointed.

"So he may not be at home. I should be sorry to miss him. However, thank you for your information. I will take the address, if I may, and if I chance to see him, I will ask him to telephone you or your wife."

"Thank you, Mr. Pons. We should be glad to hear. I am afraid his mother does worry about his lack of thought from time to time."

"Entirely natural in a parent, Mr. Rillington. Well, we must not keep you further. Thank you again for the address. Come, Parker."

Once we were outside, we took the lift to the ground floor. Pons' brow was furrowed, and his eyes were sombre.

"I do not like the look of this business, Parker."

"I am inclined to agree, Pons. There seems no doubt that it is this Mr. Rillington whose son has been kidnapped."

Solar Pons nodded, fishing his pipe out of his pocket with

his disengaged hand. He still held the brown paper parcel with its gruesome contents in his left.

"However, we must not jump to untimely conclusions, Parker."

We walked out into the May sunshine and made for the nearest Tube station at Piccadilly Circus.

"I must just take this material back to Praed Street, Parker. And tomorrow our first call must be at Charing Cross Hospital. I think we may leave young Rillington's private address over, for if he is not at the hospital or at a place known to his friends, we are unlikely to draw anything but a blank at his lodgings. However, we may reserve that as a last resort."

And he thrust the sheet of mauve-coloured notepaper into his inner pocket. Next morning, we had a hurried breakfast at 7B, served by the excellent Mrs. Johnson, and afterward took the Tube to Trafalgar Square. As we walked the few hundred yards to Charing Cross Hospital, Pons was silent and preoccupied, his empty pipe clenched tightly between his strong teeth.

At the porters' office at the hospital entrance, he sent up his card to Sir Idris Armstrong, with something scribbled on it. The porter glanced at it fleetingly.

"Sir Idris has been operating this morning, sir, but I think he's out of the operating room now."

"I will not keep him a moment," said Pons, looking casually at the people who passed back and forth in the long green corridor.

A few minutes later, the porter came back and asked Pons to accompany him, and I was left alone to stare at the green walls and the printed notices to patients and visitors. Pons was back within a quarter of an hour, rubbing his hands.

"We are in luck, Parker," he chuckled. "Sir Idris was most

helpful. He sends his compliments to you and hopes we will take sherry and a biscuit with him in his room before we depart."

"That is extremely civil of him, Pons," I mumbled. "Particularly as we have never met."

Solar Pons smiled thinly.

"I was able to do him a small service once, Parker. As he says, any friend of mine...In the meantime, he has given us *carte blanche* to look around the dissecting rooms and talk to any of young Rodney Rillington's friends as happen to be upon the premises. It is certain that he is still away and that no one at the hospital has heard of him since his disappearance."

"A bad business, Pons."

"We must just keep an open mind, Parker, and hope for the best."

And he led the way down the long, bleak corridor that led to the dissecting rooms.

4

It was a long time since I had been at Charing Cross, but nothing seemed to have changed. There were the shaded lights, the benches, the dripping sinks, the sheeted forms, the students in white coats hard at work under the eyes of a critical teacher. The atmosphere, too, must have been hard for the layman to bear, and I was inwardly amused to see Pons puffing away at his pipe furiously. He turned as I came up.

"Dr. Mecker, this is my friend, Dr. Lyndon Parker. Dr. Mecker is the registrar."

Mecker, a thin, pleasant-looking man with a small black goatee shook hands warmly.

"Pleased to meet you, doctor. I understand you are looking for Rodney Rillington. I was just telling Mr. Pons that he has not been seen for some weeks."

"You cannot throw any light on his whereabouts, then," said Solar Pons, looking at him sharply.

Mecker shook his head.

"Rillington is a promising young man. He will make a very able doctor, and his assistance was extremely valuable to me personally. He was due for some leave, but he said nothing to me. One day he was here, the next he was gone."

"I see."

Solar Pons sent a thick blue spiral of smoke up toward the skylight in the ceiling and looked at Mecker quizzically.

"Perhaps some of his friends, here?"

The registrar shrugged.

"There are Fellows and Fosdyke, yonder. Hardly friends. Acquaintances, perhaps. They may know something. You are welcome to talk to them. Rillington's best friend was young Chetwynd, but he went to St. Wilfred's some weeks ago."

"Indeed."

Solar Pons gazed at his informant through the haze of blue smoke, his mind evidently elsewhere. "Well, we may have a word with him later if we draw a blank here. St. Wilfred's is in North London, is it not?"

Dr. Mecker nodded and led the way over to one of the sinks, where two young fellows, one dark-haired, dark-bearded and dark-browed, the other sandy-haired and with a fair complexion, were rinsing instruments. Both nodded cursorily as Mecker introduced us.

"These gentlemen are looking for Rodney Rillington," Mecker explained.

He nodded affably.

"Well, I will leave you, Mr. Pons. I have much to do. If you need me further, you will find my office at the end of the corridor."

"Thank you, doctor. You have been most helpful."

Pons smiled amiably through the pipe smoke at Fellows, the bearded student.

"I believe you are a friend of young Rillington."

Fellows gazed at Pons darkly, his eyes burning sullenly. He deliberately finished rinsing the scalpel in his hand and put it in the rack.

"I don't know who told you that."

"He is not a friend, then?"

The dark-haired man shifted uneasily on one foot.

"I loathed and detested him. He and his toady Chetwynd were birds of a feather. They both left here owing me money."

"Indeed," said Pons lazily. "Is that a reason for detesting anyone? May they not still pay you back?"

The effect of Pons' words on the student was astonishing. He seemed convulsed with rage and shook his rubber-gloved fist in front of Pons' nose.

"Have a care! I am the middleweight boxing champion of the medical school."

"Really," said Solar Pons coolly. "I would not advise you to do anything foolish, or you may well need medical attention yourself."

The other student, Fosdyke, who had a frank, open face, gave a short, barking laugh. Fellows spun on his heel, glared at all of us in turn, flung down a tray of instruments into the sink with a clatter, and strode off in suppressed fury.

"What a brute, Pons!" I cried indignantly.

"He is an amiable fellow," Pons agreed, "but I fancy he would have met his match if he had crossed swords with me."

"Take no notice of him, Mr. Pons," said Fosdyke, still laughing. He advanced to shake Pons' hand.

"Fellows is a sullen brute and one of the most ill-mannered persons I have ever come across. He is cordially loathed and detested about here. I believe his hatred of Rillington stems from envy of his family's wealth."

I exchanged a sharp glance with Pons. The latter puffed blue smoke up to the skylight and regarded the student steadily through it.

"You intrigue me, Mr. Fosdyke. What is this business of owed money Fellows was speaking of?"

The young student laughed again.

"Take no notice, Mr. Pons. If Rillington and Chetwynd owed Fellows anything, it could not have been more than two or three shillings. I should imagine that Fellows once inadvertently paid their bus fares and felt he should have been reimbursed."

I could not resist a broad smile at Fosdyke—he was so open-faced and bubbling with good-humour.

"You sound as though you have had some bad experiences at the hands of Fellows yourself."

"I could tell you some things about that man you would not believe, Dr. Parker. And I am sure that Rodney will return shortly."

Solar Pons gazed at him keenly.

"What makes you say that, Mr. Fosdyke?"

"Well, there is surely nothing unusual in a third-year medical student disappearing for a few weeks. Rillington is very steady and lives a routine life, I grant you, but everyone kicks over the traces at times. Perhaps he has a girl-friend..."

"Perhaps," said Solar Pons absently. "You have been most helpful, Mr. Fosdyke."

"I am afraid I know very little, Mr. Pons. But if you talk to Chetwynd at St. Wilfred's, he should be able to tell you everything you want to know. He is his best friend, after all."

"I see. Thank you."

The young student looked at Pons quizzically.

"I hope Rodney does not owe you any money, Mr. Pons?"

Solar Pons smiled.

"No, it is nothing like that at all, Mr. Fosdyke. Just a friendly visit. Good day."

And he strode from the room before I scarcely had time to make my own *adieu*. I caught up with him in the corridor. He was still smiling, shovelling smoke from his pipe back over his shoulder furiously.

"What do you make of it, Parker?"

"It seems to me this man Fellows could have been the culprit, Pons. He hates Rillington and could have had ample opportunity to kidnap him. You heard young Fosdyke say he was envious of his comfortable background."

"Perhaps, Parker. We shall just have to reserve judgement."

"He has a foul temper, Pons, and is undoubtedly an ugly customer."

"You are certainly right there, Parker. But I fancy I could have taught him a much-needed lesson if it had come to the pinch."

"I have no doubt of that, Pons."

After our brief visit to Sir Idris, Solar Pons was in sombre mood as we walked back down in the direction of Charing Cross Station.

"All the same, we are in deep waters here, Parker. This is a sinister business, and we have only a short period left in which to find the person responsible for young Rillington's kidnapping before the time limit elapses."

I nodded, pausing to let a horse-drawn omnibus pass in front of the Charing Cross Hotel.

Solar Pons looked at me mockingly.

"What did you think of Fosdyke?"

"A little too bland for my liking, Pons. Slightly too forthcoming about Fellows and Rillington."

"Perhaps, Parker."

"Where are we going now, Pons?"

"To St. Wilfred's, of course. It is just possible that young Chetwynd will have something to add to the matter."

A short, twenty-minute journey on the Tube brought us close to our destination and after threading several bright, spacious back streets, we came to the hospital, an Edwardian brick edifice that had a cheerful, well-scrubbed appearance. Pons sent his card in to the matron by one of the orderlies, and that lady took us in person to a large recreation room on the second floor, which was full of doctors and students drinking coffee and talking shop.

Chetwynd, who had just come off the wards, proved to be a large-boned, cheerful individual with an open, pink-cheeked appearance which made him look like an overgrown schoolboy. In his white coat, with stethoscope peeping from one pocket, he appeared, in fact, like a choirboy engaged in some mischievous errand. His eyes sparkled when Solar Pons introduced himself.

"The famous detective, sir? Honoured to meet you."

"This is my friend, Dr. Lyndon Parker."

Chetwynd shook my hand warmly.

"Allow me to get you a cup of coffee, gentlemen. I am not due in to my next lecture for half an hour yet."

And he elbowed his way through the boisterous group round the canteen counter, reappearing a few moments later with two steaming mugs. He silently toasted us over the rim of his own.

"What can I do for you, gentlemen?"

"I really wanted to have a word with Rodney Rillington, and I understood you were his best friend," said Solar Pons.

Chetwynd looked puzzled.

"That is certainly correct, Mr. Pons. But I have not seen Rodney for some weeks. I understand he intended to take a short holiday in Spain. You know he is at Charing Cross, of course?"

Solar Pons nodded, his keen glance raking across the people in the crowded canteen.

"We have already been there. This is purely a personal matter. I met him at a lecture some time ago and happened to run into his father this morning. He entrusted me with a domestic message—that is all."

"I see."

Chetwynd was silent for a moment, sipping his coffee, his frank gaze fixed upon Pons' face.

"It is rather peculiar, now that you mention it, Mr. Pons. I am Rodney's closest friend, and he usually sends me a card when he is on holiday."

"You have received nothing, then?"

Chetwynd shook his head.

"Not on this occasion, Mr. Pons. I can give you Rodney's private address. I am talking about his lodgings, of course. He lives not far from me, and we often travelled to Charing Cross together. But I do not think he has been there."

"That will not be necessary, Mr. Chetwynd," said Solar Pons. "I already have the address from his father."

"Well, gentlemen, I must be off to my lecture in a moment, but if anything occurs to me, I will telephone. You are in the book?"

"Certainly, Mr. Chetwynd. And thank you for the coffee."

We watched as the strong, athletic form of Chetwynd strode out of the canteen.

"Well, he certainly knows nothing of the matter, Pons. This is extremely serious. What are we to do?"

"We have little choice, Parker."

Pons looked at me sombrely.

"As I have remarked before, time is of the essence if we are to save the boy's life. We must take the money to Charing Cross ourselves. Two further days were allowed, but I am inclined to think the matter will wait no longer than this afternoon."

5

"Do you really think this young man is still alive, Pons?"
"We can only hope so, Parker."

Solar Pons' face was grave as he sat at the table in our sitting room at 7B Praed Street. Lunch had been cleared away, and the air was blue with pipe smoke, through which the brilliant spring sunshine darted rays of gilt.

Pons had before him on the table heaped sheets of newspaper, brown paper and string, gummed adhesive tape, pen and ink, a pair of scissors, and the gruesome packages containing the severed fingers, which had been sent to Bancroft Pons' eccentric neighbour.

I pulled up my chair to the table and watched with unfeigned curiosity as Pons set to work. He first cut sheet after sheet of newspaper into strips about four inches long by three inches wide. My bewilderment mounted as the heaps grew. From time to time, Pons consulted some figures he had scrawled on a pad in front of him and put some small weights on a pair of brass scales he sometimes used for his chemical experiments. Eventually my curiosity got the better of me.

"What are you doing, Pons?"

"Can you not guess, Parker?"

I shook my head. My companion gave me a wry smile through the pipe smoke.

"I am baiting a trap, Parker. Trusting to the greed of the person who has kidnapped young Rillington. I shall address this to 'Adam Bede', leave it at Charing Cross left-luggage office, and we will just wait to see what happens."

"I see, Pons! You are making up a packet to look like a parcel of money!"

"Exactly, Parker. I called at my bank before lunch and had them weigh up a bundle of notes. They thought I was mad, but one must put up with these minor inconveniences in my profession."

"So the parcel will weigh exactly the same as that containing fifteen thousand one-pound notes, Pons?"

Solar Pons shook his head.

"That would be a little difficult to carry, Parker. Say rather, fifteen thousand pounds in five-pound notes—making due allowance for the ringers sent to Rillington, which I am returning care of the sender, as it were."

"A grim jest, Pons."

My companion frowned at me through the clouds of smoke that still hung around his head.

"But poetic justice, I think, Parker."

With satisfaction, he finished stacking the bundles of cut newspaper and wrapped them in brown paper, sealing them with the adhesive tape and then tying the packet with string. He then proceeded to put several more layers of brown paper around them, repeating the procedure each time. When that was done, he put the packages containing the fingers on top and finished doing up the bulky parcel. He sat back with a grunt.

"I think that will do nicely now."

"I do not get the point, Pons—of all these wrappings, I mean."

"Do you not, Parker? But my precautions are vital. I must do up the parcel in such a way as to make it look authentic in size and weight. At the same time, I must make it extremely difficult to open."

"But why, Pons?"

"Well, it is surely obvious, my dear fellow. Our man must not open the package when he collects it from Charing Cross, or the game is up. I am hoping he will leave it until he gets back to where he has hidden young Rillington."

"I see. Thus giving us the opportunity of following?"

Solar Pons nodded crisply.

"Exactly. I am afraid it may mean a long and weary wait at Charing Cross. And we shall have to make sure that we are unlikely to be noticed by our quarry. That may take a little ingenuity. I think our best plan would be to hire a car in the first instance."

"He will not come on foot then?"

Solar Pons shook his head.

"I think it unlikely. He will obviously be on his guard and may need to leave the station in a hurry. Besides, it is extremely difficult to keep a person captive in the metropolis, with its teeming multitudes. It is my guess that young Rillington is being held somewhere in the country—providing he is still alive."

I stared at Pons in silence as he finished addressing the parcel in heavy block capitals: ADAM BEDE ESQ., c/o LEFT-LUGGAGE OFFICE, CHARING CROSS STATION.

He consulted his watch.

"Let us see. It is now three o'clock. It will take you half an hour to hire a suitable vehicle from the garage down the street and only a few minutes more to get to Charing Cross. I think I will get Mrs. Johnson to make us some sandwiches and a thermos of coffee, which we will keep in the vehicle. They will be most useful if we have to go out of town, as we may not be able to get anything to eat this evening."

"That sounds entirely satisfactory, Pons."

My companion smiled thinly.

"I do not think you need fear starvation, my dear fellow. You look remarkably solid to me. But it is as well to be comfortable. And I think you had better hire the car for two days. Tomorrow is Wednesday, and we shall not need it beyond that, for Rillington may be beyond earthly help if my plan fails."

He paused a moment and looked at me with his deep-set eyes, in which little flecks of anger were stirring.

"And bring your revolver. It has proved remarkably persuasive in the past."

6

The hiss of escaping steam was deafening as I hurried after Pons through the crowds at Charing Cross Station, the air filled with the noise of engines, the sharp sound of hurrying feet, and the slam of carriage doors. Pons was already at the left-luggage counter when I arrived, talking to a lugubrious looking railway employee.

"I don't know, sir," he said, scratching his head. "So long as it isn't against Southern regulations."

"It is nothing like that," Pons explained patiently. "I want to leave this parcel. A gentleman will be along for it later. He will not have a ticket. All I want you to do is to let him have it."

The man squinted at the package Pons had put on the counter.

"Mr. Bede? Mr. Adam Bede."

Pons nodded.

"That is correct. Will you be on duty for the rest of today?"

"Until midnight, sir."

"Very well. All I want you to do is this. When the gentleman comes to collect the parcel, he will have no ticket. I want you to listen to his explanation, grumble a little, and then let him have it. He will, of course, identify himself as Adam Bede."

The man still looked dubious.

"Very well, sir. Some sort of joke, is it?"

"Something like that. When you give him the parcel, I want you to take out your handkerchief as if to blow your nose. When the man has his back to you, wave it in the air like this."

Pons took out his own handkerchief and waved it above his head. The attendant looked astonished.

"Like that, sir? Very well."

"And please remember it. It is most important. A white hand-kerchief, mind. Not a coloured one, which would not stand out very well."

"Very good, sir. Like this?"

The man had produced a somewhat grubby article, which Pons pronounced himself satisfied with.

"Excellent. Here is two guineas for your trouble."

The man's eyes opened.

"Thank you, sir. That is most generous. I should be able to remember that all right."

Solar Pons chuckled as we hurried away, this time across the concourse toward the stationmaster's office.

"I am not quite sure I understand, Pons."

"Tut, Parker. That man's signal will merely increase the chances of our securing our man. Once he disappears among the crowd, we are finished. He may go down the steps to Villiers Street, onto one of the platforms, or out by any of the main entrances. Or even into the Tube station."

"I see, Pons."

Solar Pons had halted and was watching the passing crowds in an abstracted fashion, though in reality his keen eyes were probing about the station.

"So we must be concealed nearby, ready to follow whichever way he goes. That is the major problem."

I gave Pons a worried glance.

"Supposing he has already seen us? He may have been watching while we went to the left-luggage office."

Solar Pons shook his head.

"A one in a million chance, Parker. No one in his right senses would maintain a twelve-hour watch on that office, even for fifteen thousand pounds. Apart from being too conspicuous, it would be pointless. He could come any time, but he would soon spot anyone hanging about the left-luggage area. So we have to be well away from there, though well placed for a signal."

"I do not see how we are to do it, Pons."

"Come, Parker, it is not so very difficult. We will just have a discreet word with the stationmaster."

That gentleman received us in his private office as soon as Pons sent a clerk in with his card, and when Pons had explained his errand and the necessity for discretion, he proved most helpful.

"There is an office at the back here, Mr. Pons," he said. "It can be reached by a staircase near the booking office and opens into the interior of the station. From the window you should be able to see the left-luggage area. I will conduct you there myself."

"You are most kind."

"Not at all, Mr. Pons."

The stationmaster led the way out toward the main concourse of Charing Cross and, ushering us through a panelled door, led us up a staircase into an empty office lit by gas lamps with green shades. At Pons' request, he turned out the lamps, leaving us in semi-darkness. As I approached the glass window behind Pons, I could see that we were high up toward the station roof. Down below, the hurrying crowds were plainly visible through the grimy window. Beyond the bookstall the ticket office area was in clear view, though at a considerable distance.

"I will see that you are not disturbed, Mr. Pons."

"Many thanks, Mr. Ironside."

"Mr. Pons. Doctor. You will find me in my office should you require me further."

The stationmaster bowed himself out, and I turned back to Pons. He had taken a pair of binoculars from the leather case slung round his neck and was swivelling the eyepieces.

"Excellent, Parker. This should do the trick nicely."

He pulled up a high stool from one of the desks and adjusted the eyepieces again, resting the heavy binoculars on the thick wooden bar of the window frame.

"I suggest we take turns. Half an hour each, perhaps. It is too tiring otherwise."

"Very well, Pons. Whatever you say."

He motioned me forward, and I looked through the binoculars, swivelling the focusing ring gently. The lenses were so powerful that I could see every detail of the cloakroom attendant to whom we had spoken, just as though I were standing only a yard away. Pons gave me a glance of satisfaction.

"I trust you see the practicality of the scheme, Parker."

"Indeed, Pons. In fact, I think I could read the time by the man's watch."

"No doubt."

Solar Pons smiled a slow smile and took the binoculars from me.

"I will stand the first watch. It might be a good idea to take some refreshment while we are at the station. It could be a long vigil. We will leave the coffee and sandwiches for tonight."

"An excellent idea, Pons. I have some chocolate here in my pocket. And I will just slip down to the buffet for some beer."

Solar Pons' eyes were twinkling as he turned back to the binoculars.

"I can see that my training is bearing fruit. You are becoming quite the seasoned campaigner."

◌ 7

I shifted my cramped position at Pons' touch on my shoulder and moved over, relinquishing the binoculars with satisfaction. I blinked, clearing the water from my eyes.

"This concentration is difficult, Pons."

"Is it not, Parker? But necessary, I fear, if we are to prevent a major tragedy. I am grateful to you for your invaluable assistance."

"You are too good, Pons."

It was five o'clock, and we had drawn a blank so far. Pons made himself more comfortable at the stool, adjusting the eye-pieces of the binoculars to suit his own powerful eyesight, his keen, feral face alert and tireless. I poured a glass of beer and handed it to him, moving back to the desk to pour myself one. I drank slowly, closing my eyes, the watering gradually ceasing.

Down below, the muffled noises of the great station went on incessantly—the hiss of steam, the rumble of wheels on steel rails as trains entered and departed, the beat of countless footsteps as the crowds ebbed and flowed beneath our vantage point high up in the dusty office, the sharper clatter of luggage trolleys snaking their way across the concourse, and the mumble of hundreds of voices, which echoed under the great metal and glass roof like the distant thunder of the sea.

"Mankind is a fascinating study, Parker."

"Perhaps, Pons, but I find it a little overpowering *en masse.*"

"There is something in what you say, my dear fellow. Just take my glass, will you?"

I crossed over to Pons and took it from him, and as I did so, he gave a muffled exclamation.

"Hullo! This looks like something."

There was an urgency in his voice that was unmistakable. I crossed instantly to his side. He handed me the binoculars.

"The man at the counter."

The bluish image in the eyepieces blurred and then came sharply into focus as I adjusted the knurled ring. I saw a burly man in a black raincoat who was engaged in deep argument with the railway employee we had interviewed at the left-luggage counter. On the wooden barrier between them was a large brown paper parcel, which I had no difficulty in recognising as that which Pons had addressed to 'Adam Bede'. I gave a startled exclamation, and then the man turned in the course of his argument, revealing a dark, bearded face.

"Why, Pons, the man is..."

But Solar Pons was already at my side, his strong fingers digging into my arm. I just had time to see that the man had picked up the parcel and was turning away when Pons took the binoculars from me.

"That is the signal, Parker! Our friend is waving his handkerchief. Excellent!"

I waited, straining my eyes to pick out the man, but he had disappeared in the restlessly ebbing and flowing crowds. There was a brief pause and then a sigh of relief from Pons.

"All is well, Parker. He is making for the station entrance. Quickly! There is not a second to lose."

He had thrust the binoculars back into their case and was impatiently opening the staircase door before I had turned to follow. I panted down the staircase behind him. When I reached the street, Pons was already getting into our hired car, and I tumbled behind the wheel, starting the engine at Pons' urgent request.

"All is well, Parker. Our man got into the driving seat of that tourer over there. He is quite alone. Ah, as I thought, the parcel wrappings have defeated him. He is taking the bait!"

Even as he spoke, blue exhaust smoke erupted from the vehicle parked a dozen yards in front of us, and it glided from the station entrance toward Trafalgar Square. I eased our own car out, keeping several vehicles behind. It was not difficult maintaining our quarry in view, as the tourer was a light cream colour and stood out from the rest of the traffic.

It went only a few yards before turning left down Northumberland Avenue toward the Victoria Embankment. As we came in sight of the Thames, a breeze ruffling the brown muddy surface of the river with its strings of barges, the driver of the tourer signalled a right turn, and we followed along toward the Gothic silhouette of the Houses of Parliament. He turned left at Big Ben, and Pons gave a muffled exclamation of satisfaction.

"Excellent, Parker. He is going south of the river."

The traffic was thinning a little now, and we rumbled swiftly through the Elephant and Castle area and on to New Cross. I still kept several vehicles between me and our quarry, and I felt sure that our man did not realise he was being followed. Pons was silent, his strong teeth clamped around the stem of his pipe, aromatic blue smoke wreathing over his shoulder.

The tourer went straight on south without slacking, except for obstructions and traffic signals, and it was obvious that the driver knew every inch of the route. I was becoming a little worried and could not help voicing my fears to Pons.

"You are sure this is right, Pons?"

"Certainly, Parker. This is our man. He is making for the country, as I felt sure he would. As for the vehicle, it is certainly the same one we followed from Charing Cross. I have not taken my eyes off it for a moment, and I have noted the license number."

Solar Pons smiled thinly.

"No, Parker, you need not worry on that score. And we can always trace the driver through the vehicle registration—though I fear in that event we would have to admit defeat, and young

Rillington's life would be forfeit. So we must not lose contact under any circumstances."

Certainly the vehicle in front went on unhesitatingly, as though the driver had no suspicion of being followed. Circumstances were on our side in any event, for I had noticed that the vehicle, being an all-weather tourer with a canvas top, had only a small mica window at the rear which was heavily discoloured and cracked and which would surely have prevented the driver from seeing following vehicles in any great detail in his rear-view mirror.

We were passing through Bromley, and the late May sunshine was gilding the rooftops with gold before Pons broke the silence again.

"What did I tell you, Parker? Kent or Sussex, most certainly. We have another hour or so of daylight. My guess is he would not wish to be more than two hours' by car or an hour by rail from London."

"Why do you think he used a car today, Pons?"

"He is a frightened man, Parker. There would be less difficulty escaping in an emergency than if he had to rely on public transportation."

"Did you see his face, Pons?"

Solar Pons nodded, briefly taking his eye off the cream tourer, which was now five cars in front of us.

"We will just await events, Parker, and try not to anticipate."

He remained silent as the pursuit continued. I must confess my throat was dry and my hands trembled a little on the steering wheel as I considered the importance of our mission and the possible consequences of failure for young Rillington. My one fear was that there might be some trouble with our car, but my faith in the garage from which I had rented it was justified.

The petrol tank was full when we left town, and we had not yet used more than two gallons, and the engine was running smoothly and without difficulty. We were now passing through Sevenoaks, on narrow, winding roads, and I had only a brief glimpse of the magnificence of Knole House, behind its screen of trees across the parkland to the left of the road, before it seemed we were plunging down the leafy steepness of Riverhill.

The light was dying a little from the sky, and there came an agreeable aroma of cut grass as we penetrated deeper into the richness of the Kent countryside. The cream tourer went straight on south, and my worries were increasing as it showed no sign of slackening speed. We were on the outskirts of Tunbridge Wells now, and it was almost seven o'clock.

The green domes of the Opera House were in sight when the driver of the tourer signalled a right-hand turn and went along the top of the Common in the Rusthall direction, the elegant placidity of Tunbridge Wells spread out to our left.

"I do not think it will be much further, Parker," said Solar Pons with satisfaction.

The tourer went on still, without hesitating, and soon we were proceeding up and downhill, on the Crowborough road. There were two vehicles between us and our quarry, and I still felt that he could not possibly realise he had been followed from London.

Pons gave a muffled exclamation, and at the same instant the tourer turned left onto a side road, bordered by dark trees.

"Sussex, Parker," said my companion crisply. "My bet is Ashdown Forest. It is isolated enough for his purposes."

"It looks as though you are right, Pons," I said, for we were now travelling down a steep hill with dark evergreen trees sweeping to the edges of the road. There were few vehicles on the road and in fact only one large car, a Bentley, between us and the convertible, so I gradually slackened speed and drew back so as not to make our quarry suspicious.

When we rounded the next bend, however, I was stupefied to see nothing but the dark green Bentley in the long stretch of road before us. I cast an embarrassed glance at my companion.

"I have lost him, Pons!"

"I think not, Parker," said Solar Pons with a wry smile. "He has merely turned off at that farm road a few hundred yards back. Kindly turn the car here."

I did as Pons directed and soon found the road that, as Pons had indicated, was the only place the tourer could have gone. Pons put his finger to his lips to enjoin caution.

"I think we will get out, Parker, and proceed on foot. Sound carries a long way out here. You have your revolver ready?"

I produced it from my inner pocket and handed it to him while I parked the car. When I had stopped the engine, we could still faintly hear the progress the tourer was making down the narrow lane. I took the weapon from Pons, threw off the safety catch, and followed him down the side road, which wound about the dark trees. There was still a lot of light in the sky, but it was twilight here, because the trees hedged the track in so closely.

We had walked about 300 yards in this fashion, taking care to keep on the thick grass at the side of the lane, when I became aware that the distant engine noise had stopped. Pons had a faint smile of satisfaction on his face when we left the road and eased through a small grove of firs. As the undergrowth thinned, I could see that the lane led only to some tumble-down farm buildings. The tourer was parked in front of a dilapidated barn. The road simply petered out in the dirt yard of the farm.

"We have him, Parker," Solar Pons whispered exultantly. "Providing he does not open that parcel for another minute or so, he cannot possibly start his engine and turn around before we reach the barn."

I hurried at his heels as Pons made for the door of the structure, enjoining caution. My companion stopped at the large double doors, into which a smaller entrance was set, and put his finger to his lips. He listened intently for a few moments, his eye fastened to a crack in the rough planking. Then, inch by inch, he eased open the door. I followed him through the narrow gap and waited while Solar Pons closed it carefully behind us.

It was dark in there, and I waited for my eyes to adjust to the light, conscious of heavy footsteps overhead. Pons was moving again, skilfully avoiding heavy beams and pieces of farm machinery that were set about the floor. There was a massive oak staircase leading upward into the shadow, and Pons mounted it carefully, testing each step with painstaking care. But the man we had followed here was obviously oblivious to any tiny noise we might have made, for we could hear his heavy progress above us, as he paced to and fro across the rough plank floor.

Then a light flared above, illuminating the crudely partitioned corridor in which we found ourselves. The upper half of the barn had evidently once been used to store hay and vegetables, because the left-hand side had been divided into bays. There was an open trapdoor in the floor, at one side, down which the hay and other materials evidently had been forked.

The light was shining from a bay at the far end, and I eased forward to join Pons behind a piece of sheeted farm machinery, from which we could obtain a clear view into the shadowy chamber ahead of us. I shall never forget the sight that met my eyes.

There was an oil lamp burning on top of an upended packing case, which cast a wan, unearthly glow on the drama taking place before us. In a corner, on a filthy bed of straw, lay a young man, manacled by the legs to a strong chain stapled into an immense oak beam that ran at right angles to the floor. He was pale and unshaven, his eyes burning with feverish intensity. Near him, just within the arc allowed him by the length of the chain, were a wash bowl, a water jug, and a bucket.

On his right side were a bowl, a drinking cup, bottles, a loaf of bread, and packets of food. The young man moved painfully on the straw, the chain clanking as he eased his position.

"Just how much longer are you going to keep me here?"

The voice was defiant still but weak and uncertain from fear and isolation in this remote place. The figure hunched on a stool at the packing-case table shifted impatiently. I recognised the form as that of the man we had followed from Charing Cross Station. He still wore the dark raincoat, but now, in addition, he wore a black canvas hood, which completely concealed his face and head. He looked inexpressibly sinister in the dim light of the barn.

The chained man's gaoler had his head bent over the table again, and I could hear the rustling of paper as he impatiently tore at the parcel Pons had so carefully prepared. I turned to Pons, but his alert, feral face was concentrated absolutely on the scene before us. The noise of tearing paper went on. The hooded figure rose to its feet and was savagely concentrating on its task. There was rage and frustration in every line of his figure as he tore at the wrappings.

Then they came free, and he bent forward eagerly over the

loosened paper. There was a faint rustling sound as he opened the enclosure. Then a cry so anguished and frustrated echoed around the dim apartment, followed by a bellow of rage, that I instinctively started up, bringing the barrel of my revolver to a level position.

"What does this mean?" a muffled voice, distorted by anger and shock, croaked from the depths of the hood.

"It means that the game is over!" said Solar Pons coolly, stepping from his place of concealment.

The hooded figure whirled, the packet containing the severed fingers falling to the floor. At the same moment, the parcel dropped from the table, bursting on impact and scattering the cut sheets of newspaper that Pons had so carefully arranged to look like a package of banknotes. The man in the hood snarled, turning quickly to snatch up a heavy iron bar leaning against the wall. He rushed forward to beat Pons down.

I fired once, the crack sounding deafening in the confines of the bay. The hooded figure screamed, clutching with his right hand at the shattered left elbow, from which blood was spouting. The bar fell and bounced away among the straw. Before I could get to him the hooded man jumped away, gave a hoarse cry, and tumbled through the open trapdoor onto the floor of the barn below.

"Quick, Parker!" Solar Pons shouted. "Young Rillington will be well enough for the moment."

He ran down the oak steps with incredible rapidity, and I followed as quickly as I was able. The groaning figure that lay sprawled in the straw was badly injured, but it was evident from my necessarily hurried examination that his wounds were not fatal. The hood had fallen clear in his fall, and when Pons had opened the wide double door of the barn, the fading light streamed into the interior, revealing the burning eyes and bearded face.

I had finished bandaging the patient's arm and was trying to make him comfortable when Pons, who had been standing by, a stern expression on his face, bent down. The dark beard and hairpiece came away in his hands. I gazed stupefied at the sullen features of young Chetwynd.

"Heavens, Pons!" I exclaimed. "I do not understand."

"It would not be the first time, Parker," Solar Pons chuckled. "You were so obviously set upon Fellows. Chetwynd here, no doubt depended on that, as he knew the two men were on unfriendly terms. You made the elementary mistake, Parker, of looking for the obvious when seeking the enemy of young Rillington. A man of such sullen ill-temper as Fellows would hardly have been responsible. He is a man of avowed hostility to the kidnapped young man, the trail would have led straight to him. Revenge for imagined slights, not kidnapping profit, would have been his motivating force, and he would have been far more subtle. I was looking from the beginning for someone close to Rillington—one who had opportunity and personal knowledge of his habits and movements."

"So you were directed to Chetwynd from the beginning, Pons?"

"Not quite, Parker, but he was a little too open and frank. And I fancy that such a distinctively bearded character as Fellows would hardly have gone openly to Charing Cross Station on such a potentially dangerous mission. Therefore, as soon as I caught sight of a bearded man at the luggage counter, I came to the conclusion that he was disguised."

He stood back, his deep-set eyes boring into Chetwynd's own.

"What was it? Racing, cards, women? It is usually something of the sort."

Chetwynd slumped forward with a groan, tears running in long rivulets down his face.

"Do not be too hard on me, Mr. Pons. I meant Rodney no harm and would have released him without a scratch. I was in for nearly five thousand pounds. There is a girl I hoped to marry, and I spent a good deal of money in impressing her family. I borrowed at extortionate rates and then tried to win the money back at gambling clubs."

"It is the old story," said Solar Pons reflectively. "But kidnapping and extortion are among the vilest of crimes. Did you give one thought to young Rillington's suffering?"

"To say nothing of the barbarous mutilation!" I said indignantly.

Solar Pons shook his head.

"I think you will find, if you look carefully, Parker, that young Mr. Rillington has all his fingers. I saw from the beginning that the kidnapping was the work of a rank amateur. The elementary mistake of sending the demand for money to the wrong man— by the merest coincidence both Rillingtons live in the St. John's Wood area; the wrapping of the severed fingers in an old copy of *The Lancet*; and the inept demand for fifteen thousand pounds."

I looked at my companion in puzzlement.

"I do not follow you, Pons."

"Tut, Parker, it is simplicity itself. Any professional kidnapper would have demanded half a million pounds of such a wealthy parent if he was going to risk his liberty for such an odious crime. I had long ago come to the conclusion that we must seek our man from among Rillington's close companions—ones who had access to dissecting rooms and could easily amputate a corpse's finger to give an added edge to their menacing notes."

"But such a close friend, Pons."

"That would not be so very difficult, Parker, particularly when the man in question had such a ready-made enemy as Fellows who, I must confess, impressed me most unfavourably. Did you chloroform Rillington one dark night, or hit him over the head?"

His question was addressed to the white-faced man at our feet. Chetwynd swallowed once or twice and then nodded.

"I dined with him one evening. He had a great deal to drink. I said good-night and went down to the street door alone. I left it unlatched and crept back. I put on the hood and a dark rain-coat and chloroformed him as he lay half-insensible at the table. I had the car at the door and brought him straight here. I had prepared the scheme months ago."

Solar Pons' face was impassive as he stared at Chetwynd.

"And these farm buildings?"

"Derelict, Mr. Pons. I rented them under an assumed name. No one comes here. I came down every other day to see that all was well with Rillington. I swear that he would not have come to any harm."

"You will have to convince the court of that, Mr. Chetwynd," said Pons grimly.

He turned to me.

"Thank God it has all turned out well, Parker. And now, I think you may safely leave this villain to his thoughts and direct your professional skills toward a more worthy end. There is not a moment to lose in returning young Rodney Rillington to the bosom of his family."

SOLAR PONS

7B, PRAED STREET
PADDINGTON, LONDON, W. 2   AMBASSADOR 10000